Don't Bullshit Me Johnny

Jon Ferguson

Huge Jam
2024

First published Huge Jam,
Gravenhurst, England 2024

ISBN: 978-1-916604-24-7

1

It didn't take long for Daddy to die. True, it took longer than it did for Mommy, but that's not saying much. Mommy got her "it-doesn't-look-good-Mrs-Winger" diagnosis and was in the coffin three months later. In Daddy's case, after the doctor told him that he "had some bad news", he saw each of the four seasons one more time. Fortunately, Switzerland is a good place to see them.

Mommy's buried in the Pleasant Hill cemetery. Pleasant Hill is a town of about thirty thousand in the rolling hills outside of San Francisco. Daddy's not buried anywhere. He flew away.

I'm really not sure why Mommy went into the ground and Daddy up in the air. (I shouldn't say "up in the air" because if there's one thing Daddy taught me it's that there is no "up" or "down" in the universe, but only in the human head...) As far as I know, Mommy never asked to be buried, and Daddy sure as hell never told me he wanted to go up in smoke. But, given that we were a family of three, Daddy decided for Mommy and I decided for Daddy. Who will decide for me has yet to be determined. Maybe I should write an official signed and sealed document explaining exactly how I want to be dealt with when the day comes, but I'm only eighteen years old and not in the mood to think much about my own demise. Mommy went underground when I was eight, Daddy got smoked last year, so I figure I should give Laura Jezabel Winger a little time to relax before we think about how we should dispose of her carcass.

So why did Mommy get buried and Daddy burned? The fact that Mommy died in California and Daddy in Switzerland accounts for something. There's a whole lot more room for dead people in America. America's a big place. In Switzerland real estate is scarce. (Did you know you can fit Switzerland into California ten times – or something like that? I calculated it once in geography class.) I don't know if I could have found a spot for Daddy even if I had wanted to. And there was no way I was going to pack his body on ice and fly it back to America. I just had a hunch that he preferred spending eternity mingling with the moon and stars to being breakfast, lunch and dinner for worms and maggots. Plus, he hated small elevators. I just didn't have the heart to put him in a two-meter box and close the lid…forever. Not only that, but just before he died, my English teacher at school had us read a story by Roald Dahl called "The Way Up to Heaven" where a nasty filthy-rich husband in New York gets stuck in the elevator in his fancy house and his wife knowingly leaves him there while she goes to Paris for six weeks to visit her grandchildren. I couldn't think of a worse death than being stuck in a small elevator with no food or water and no possibility of lying down. Yeah, Daddy could have at least reclined in a coffin, but I just couldn't do it. I told the funeral guys to light the match.

Daddy's been dead almost a year. I actually wrote my first book two years ago when I was sixteen. I'm quite sure it was Mommy's death that stimulated me to write "Don't Bullshit Me Daddy". Why do people write? Because they've got all kinds of stuff inside them that has to come out one way or another. Daddy used to say the same thing about sex. Sex for men anyway. He said that pornography was just a way of helping lonely men get rid of all those spermatozoids building up inside. Well, seeing Mommy shrivel up like an albino prune and die when I was eight years old left a few things simmering in my little noggin. Eight years later and bang, a book. With Daddy, the soup only needed to simmer for a little more than a year. There was no way I could have written anything during the first few months after his death, but now I feel like I have to write something. If I don't I'll go crazy. Daddy did kind of a Hemingway thing in that he borrowed a friend's gun and blew his own brains out. It was kind of ironic because Daddy hated guns with a passion. He used to say that U.S. presidents were all a bunch of pussies for not standing up to the National Rifle Association and all the idiots who say the Constitution is a divine document and that God guaranteed the right for people in the ghetto to shoot each other whenever they got "dissed" or otherwise pissed off with somebody in the neighborHOOD. Daddy thought this was some of the biggest bullshit in the history of mankind. One night at dinner not long before he died, he said, "Would Jesus have carried a gun! Hell no he wouldn't have carried a gun! All these goddamned Christians saying it's their God-given right to have a gun in their glove-compartment or their jacket pocket! If Jesus were alive today he'd be the leader of every anti-gun group in America! Except that he WOULDN'T BE AMERICAN! He'd say a passport was as bad as a gun. Guns kill and passports make people into chauvinistic morons! Every American who thinks God watches over America and not the rest of the world should have his passport confiscated! Every pro-gun lobbyist should see what it feels like to get shot in the chest by some cocaine infested would-be rap star!" … It was one of the few times I really saw Daddy pissed off. And then he started telling me about a member of some big basketball star's family who had just been shot and killed in Chicago. It was the month of March and the news announced that over three hundred people had already been murdered that year by guns in Barack Obama's hometown (well, adopted hometown). "That's a hundred a month!" Daddy shouted. "Three a day! In one city! What are there… 10,000 gun murders a year in America? And no politician has the balls to stand up and say 'God has changed His fucking mind. Guns are evil! Guns are bad! God told me He wants guns BANNED!'" Then he compared that to the Vietnam War. He said in the whole eight or nine years in Vietnam 50,000 U.S soldiers were killed. Twice as many people were killed by guns in the streets of America. People and politicians were demonstrating all over the country about Vietnam. But guns in the street? No, no, "guns don't kill; people kill" the right-wingers (funny…my name is "Winger"!) chirp. Let the sons-a-bitches all shoot each other! That's God's will!!!…Anyway, Daddy wondered how in the hell could somebody be as hip to the jive as Obama and not want guns banned? Politics, of course. But how sad. And how ironic that Daddy used a gun to end his life. The difference is that Daddy blew his own brains out because he was suffering too much. The ghetto guys blow somebody else's brains out probably because they're suffering too much. But, like Daddy used to say, that's a story that goes back as far as the glorious slave trade days (now there's another chapter in American history where God must have put his baton down and stopped directing the divinely-inspired Founding Fathers)…and probably farther if you think about it. In fact, the older I get the more I'm starting to think that every story goes back and back and back to the beginning of time, but since I don't believe there was a beginning of time and people are too lazy or dumb to go back more than ten minutes or ten months or ten centuries, all stories are really just kind of diarrhetic bullshit. (I had to look that word up - "diarrhetic", not "bullshit". There were actually three possible adjectives coming from diarrhea: diarrheal, diarrheic, and diarrhetic. Why I chose the last one, I'll never know…I guess it sounded the most solid…or do the grammar books say "solidest"?) But I'm getting sidetracked again. I always get sidetracked these days…

So why am I writing another book? Simple answer: I need to. I have to. If I don't, I'll go crazy. My head will explode. Why do heads explode? Ideas? Feelings? Blood clots? Rotten grey matter? Electric currents? Gun shots?

And hey, it's an exciting time to be writing a book. Mitt Romney and Barack Obama are going to have a three-month boxing match. I can't think of a more perfect billing card: the lily-white Mormon in the white trunks versus the half-black guy who's probably a closet atheist (at least agnostic) in the grey trunks! Mormons didn't use to let black - or even half-black – people be priests in their church because one of their sacred books says that they – Blacks – were "cursed" with black skin for doing some sinful shit a few thousand years ago in some nasty corner of God's lovely earth. Talk about paying for your father's sins! I wonder if ravens and crows were cursed with black feathers because some bird fertilized the wrong egg a few million years ago! (How do birds make babies anyway? I must have been dreaming when my old biology teacher Mrs. Herrmann was explaining that little piece of infinite wisdom!) It was only recently - like 1978 - that the Mormon Prophet, Seer, and Revelator finally declared that God had told him that it was time to change the rule and finally let Black people be full citizens in the church. That's really what they call him, "Prophet, Seer, and Revelator"...I say "him" because there has never been a "her" in the hundred and eighty years since the church got started by Joe Smith and there probably won't be a "her" for the next hundred and eighty years! (My computer just underlined Revelator in red...I looked it up in my Big Fat American Heritage Dictionary...It's not even a word...Revealer is a word...But I swear that's what the Mormons call the top dog in their church...PROPHET, SEER, AND REVELATOR!) (I'll explain how I know all this crap about Mormons in a second...) Anyway, women – all women...black, white, green, pink, purple, orange, slightly tanned, deeply richly tanned, etc. - still can't hold what the Mormons call the priesthood. But really, why would they want to? Why would anybody want to? Why would any feminist want to be like men? Why would anybody want to be a priest in a church that didn't let Black people have full rights for 150 years and also says that you'll fry in hell if you drink tea, coffee, or wine!...The same crap about God changing his mind happened with polygamy. When the church got rolling in the mid-1800s men could have all the wives they wanted. (Oddly women couldn't have all the husbands they wanted, but this must have had something to do with the same strange quirk in nature that has modern men watching dumb vacuous pornography a thousand times more often than women. In fact, I read an article today that said that men produce one hundred and sixty-five million sperm cells every day. 165,000,000! That might explain something...And that's just in ONE gonad!) In about 1890 the American government made polygamy illegal. A couple of months later God agreed! Imagine that!!!

So how do I know all this junk about the Mormon church? Simple. After my black (I hate the words "black" and "white" – there are no black Black people and no white White people on the damn earth!…even albinos aren't WHITE!…they're off-white…kind of a pinkish cream) boyfriend Cherif, I had a white boyfriend named Chuck who happened to be a Mormon. His father worked for a big American company and got transferred to Switzerland. At first he tried to convert me to his religion, but little by little I think I started converting him out of his religion. He would tell me all these stories about Joe Smith seeing God and God hiding gold plates in some mountain in New York and polygamy and Blacks not being able to hold the priesthood and everything, and I would ask him a million questions (most of which he had absolutely no answer for) and little by little I think he started to realize how crazy all these stories were. But Chuckie and I are burnt toast now, so it doesn't matter. And really, should I care what he believes? By the time we split up, I thought maybe he needed his religion to survive. I guess religion is kind of like legs for a lot of people walking through the muddy river of life; it holds them up, keeps them from drowning when that current gets fast and furious.

2

I just reread Chapter 1. Maybe I was a little mean to the Mormons. But it's fun to be mean sometimes. Not really mean mean, but just kind of playful mean. But now I'm going to be nice. I'm going to count my blessings. Chuckie used to always say we should count our blessings. So I'm going to get on my knees and thank the universe for letting me be alive. Hey, it's true. I'm an extremely lucky person. Daddy left me lots of money. Lots and lots. He was a professor at a big-time business school. It's ridiculous to be eighteen years old and never had a job and have lots of money. But that's what happens when you're an only child and your parents both get knocked off. Bang. Bang. No Mommy. No Daddy. But lots of Uncle Francs and Aunt Dollars. And an apartment. And a car. I don't even know how to drive yet and I've got a Mazda downstairs in the garage. Daddy had a master's degree in philosophy and a doctorate in business so people thought he knew what he was talking about. His specialty was business ethics. He called it, "How to get rich without screwing over too many people in the process". He said that once the human race decided not to live in grass huts and tee-pees anymore, business became inevitable. Daddy had nothing against grass huts and tee-pees and he also had nothing against business. Two roads, same result: we all die. It just depends on how you want to live. That was his idea anyway. He said there was no solution, no real right way or wrong way. There were different ways. Maybe some ways were a little better than other ways, but somebody was always going to have the short end of the stick. A thousand times I heard Daddy say that the world was not fair, and to think it would be or should be was the sign of a dumb mind. Someone would always have power. If it wasn't dinosaurs, it was lions; if it wasn't lions, it was Caesars and Napoleons; if it wasn't Italians, it was Spaniards; if it wasn't Spaniards, it was French; if it wasn't French, it was Americans, English or the Chinese. Nothing was steering the ship in the direction of some glorious garden where everybody would be happy eating strawberries and cream all day. The world was a horror house and a whore house, not necessarily in that order. Babies get made and struggle to survive…to eat and/or get eaten. What a world!

Most kids my age don't really think about all this crap. The only ones I know who do are ones whose mommy or daddy got killed in Bosnia or Rwanda or who watched other people get killed in places like Bosnia or Rwanda. Is it good to think about this stuff when you're eighteen years old? Shouldn't you be thinking about whether or not Johnny Depp still loves Vanessa Paradis, or how cool Puff Daddy's new Ferrari is, or whether Billy loves you, or if your nose is the right shape, or if your underpants are the right brand and your boobs or biceps are big enough? Isn't that what eighteen-year-olds should be thinking about? Who knows? Who's to say what "deep" thinking is anyway? Is deep thinking really deep? Thinking about stuff is no guarantee of anything. I'll bet a lot of deep thinkers are shallow people. Maybe thinking about life and death and suffering and planetary injustice is the sign of a sick mind, a mind that can't soar to great heights and fly above all the blood and guts…If Mommy and Daddy hadn't died, maybe I'd be a pom-pom girl at Pleasant Hill High. Maybe I only think about this stuff because Mommy and Daddy kicked the bucket prematurely. Actually Daddy didn't really die early…not on a world scale…and Mommy lived longer than most people in the Middle Ages did. So why do I think about the world being a whore horror house or a horror whore house? I guess Daddy did have a lot to do with it. But he wasn't the type to rant and rave and throw bombs at people. He was rarely mad at things. Oh, every now and then like with the gun worshippers, but in general he treated people like he treated the weather. He never got mad at the weather, even when it rained for a few days in a row. He used to say, "We need rain. No rain, no life. Simple as that!" And then he'd say, "Why should I care about the weather? It doesn't care about me; I don't care about it." He observed people like he observed the weather. It was all one big flying circus speeding to nowhere. He always did like that Beatles song "Nowhere Man"…

You know, I miss the hell out of Daddy. And the reason I miss him is that I don't really have anybody to talk to anymore. Maybe that's why I'm writing this book. To have somebody to talk to. When I come home from school and turn on the TV, the stupid machine only makes me lonely. It does all the talking. When I try to say something it just keeps on babbling. It never listens to me. It doesn't care about me. Why should I care about it? Just like Daddy said about the weather.

One thing I thought was really funny was how Daddy was a teacher in a business school and yet he himself was very bad for business because he never bought anything. He said he had everything he wanted. He didn't care about a big house or fancy furniture or cars or clothes. He didn't play the stock market. He didn't wear a watch or a ring. He didn't even have an iPhone or an iPad. He was a horrible consumer. The only thing he ever bought was wine at his favorite wine store. But even then, he'd always say you could get very good wine for fifteen or twenty francs a bottle.

That was Daddy. The only one I'll ever have. I was the only daughter he'll ever have. When I think about it, we were both kind of lucky.

3

Yesterday I went for a walk, and not because I had nothing to do. I had lots to do and going for a walk was one of them. I had school crap. I had to buy groceries. I had to go to the post office to pay some bills (nobody else is going to pay them). I promised I'd go see my friend Marcel Monnet to help him with an English composition. But walks are like writing this book: if I don't do them I go crazy. I started taking walks with Daddy after the doctor told him walking a lot might help keep him alive. We would just walk out the door of the apartment and walk, sometimes after dinner, always on weekends. We'd go any direction. North is uphill, south downhill, east and west are pretty flat. We got to know Lausanne. It lasted about six months until Daddy couldn't walk anymore. We stopped walking. He died. I started walking again. Some people jog. I walk. You see more when you walk. The slower you go, the more you see. Maybe I should crawl. Anyway, I fit yesterday's walk in between the post office and Marcel Monnet. I took the bus to the next town over – Pully - and walked up the hill to a beautiful forest with a stream going down the middle. It's spring. Everything's green and blooming. After about an hour I sat down on a log and started doing what you do when you sit on a log alone in a forest. You think about yourself…like, "Geez I'm hungry. What shall I eat for dinner?", or "I sure wish I didn't have that physics test tomorrow", or "Should I buy those shoes I saw yesterday?" That kind of crap. Well, this time it wasn't an I-me-me-my. It was an ant. An amazing ant. A champion. An Olympic medallist!!! There I was, my cute little rear end on this comfortable log looking at all the green-leafy trees changing color with the little breeze that was cruising through the forest (silver to green and green to silver) and suddenly, for whatever reason, I looked down at my feet. Near the heel of my left shoe was this reddish ant walking by with a bee. The bee wasn't walking; it was as dead as Daddy; the ant was carrying it. The bee must have weighed ten times more than the ant. At least it was ten times bigger. I watched the ant carry the bee past my shoe toward wherever it was going. I started thinking about human body-builders and weightlifters and how everybody thinks they're so strong because they can lift up three hundred pounds. But three hundred pounds is what? Maybe twice their body weight. This ant was carrying ten times its body weight and carrying it through a bumpy forest. Pound for pound it was infinitely stronger than any human. Ants are the ones who should be getting all the accolades and the gold medals! Not people!…I followed the ant for a few minutes. It kept going. Finally I had to go see Marcel.

When all is said and done, Marcel Monnet might be my best friend (for whatever reason I don't have a lot of close girl friends). You should know - or remember if you read my first book - that Marcel was the first person that I ever made love with. Looking back on it, we didn't "make love", we "made sex". I've learned that making love and making sex are two very different things. When you make sex you just want to leave or be alone when you're finished. When you make love you want to stay in the bed or on the sofa or wherever you are and hang out with the person and maybe make love again. I never loved Marcel, but since making sex with him was neither traumatic nor unforgettable, we've ended up staying friends. In fact, we're in the same class at what they call "le gymnase" here in Switzerland. The gymnase is what you do before you go to the university.

This weekend we have to write a paper for English class on Hemingway's book "Farewell to Arms". What's interesting – among other things – about "Farewell to Arms" is that the end of the book takes place right here in the city of Lausanne where we live. I don't know if that's why the teacher chose the book or not. I'll ask him. But it is fun to read something and know the places the writer is writing about. The subject the teacher gave us is: "Hemingway's writing style is very simple. What is hidden behind the simplicity?" I kind of like the subject because we can pretty much talk about whatever we want to. Yesterday was Saturday and the paper has to be in on Monday. Marcel had written his and just wanted me to correct his grammar. It only took about fifteen minutes because Marcel's English is really good because he always listens to music in English and for the past year he never wants me to talk to him in French any more. I really liked his paper because he said he didn't think Hemingway was hiding anything behind the simplicity. He said Hemingway thought love was a very simple thing: either it's there or it's not. You don't need any big analytical investigation to know if it's there; you feel it or you don't. I immediately thought that his saying this meant that he understood that I didn't love him, that that was just the way things were, and that he wasn't going to try to talk me into something that wasn't there. Of course maybe he wasn't even thinking about me. Maybe some girl I don't know about loves him and he doesn't love her. Anyway, I liked it. Maybe the teacher won't like like it because sometimes he can be kind of a pedantic snob who always wants to analyze everything and in the end you're always supposed to agree with his analysis which is why grades for such a composition are bullshit. Marcel did, however, say that in the book war is portrayed as the opposite of love in that it doesn't make any sense at all. You never know who was fighting for what or why. Mr. Fluckinger might like that.

I haven't written my paper yet. I'll do it tomorrow. I've usually got nothing to do on Sunday except go to the movies or take a walk. Tomorrow is absolutely no exception; I have NOTHING to do except write my paper. In Switzerland you only have to pass your last year at the gymnase to get into the university. It's not like America where grades and money determine whether you go to Harvard or Hayward State. Here you can go to any university you want, but almost everybody around here ends up going to the University of Lausanne because it's more convenient than going to Zurich or Fribourg or St. Gall. Plus it's in French, whereas the others are in German. (Can you imagine that tiny Switzerland has four national languages?) It doesn't matter if your grades are mediocre or perfect…everybody gets in to every university as long as he or she passes the gymnase. I think it's a good system because a lot of kids still aren't too serious about school when they're sixteen or seventeen, but get serious later. Plus it's not expensive, because every school is state financed. The only problem is that most kids stay home and live with their parents for another five years, which I don't think is really good for anybody after age eighteen. In America, after high school, you get to go a few hundred or thousand miles from your parents so you can act like an idiot and they don't know about it. Not so here. Here Mommy and Daddy hear you stumble in drunk at three in the morning and give you shit the next day. If you have a mommy and daddy, that is…

Lately, I've been wondering if I even want to go to the university? If I do, what would I want to "study"? Daddy once told me he didn't remember teachers teaching him anything. He remembered working his butt off in the library reading books and thinking like crazy, but he didn't remember learning things "in the classroom". Sometimes I think the whole idea of "choosing a major" has a tendency to make the world a dumber place instead of a smarter one. Of course it's all good for building bridges and inventing medicine to cure halitosis and that kind of thing, but the problem is people who study just engineering or chemistry or whatever, often end up rather dumb shits when it comes to thinking about all the rest of existence…if you see what I mean. Wouldn't it be better if people thought about everything — history, science, religion, art, literature, physics, ping pong, cooking, politics, basket weaving, love, poetry, toilets, child-rearing, ghettos, cars, flowers, water beetles, medicine, love, infidelity, fidelity, Chinese pottery, etc. — for a few more years until they were maybe twenty-three or twenty-four (why not their whole lives?) before they start doing just ONE thing? I guess the problem with that is that most people aren't interested in EVERY thing or even MANY things so they would probably be all bored to death and would all drop out of school and end up washing dishes at McDonald's, except McDonald's doesn't have dishes. You know what I mean. But it is kind of sad how people who are smart in one area can be real dumb in others.

The truth is that because Daddy left me all kinds of money, my continued education is a bit less important than the continued education of other kids whose parents don't have much money and who don't want to spend their lives sweeping streets or being a cashier at the Migros. But when you think about it, what the hell is wrong with sweeping the streets of being a cashier in a grocery store? SOMEBODY HAS TO DO IT! SOMEBODY

HAS TO SWEEP THE DAMN STREETS AND SOMEBODY HAS TO BE A CASHIER IN THE MIGROS! SO WHY DO PEOPLE DENEGRATE THESE JOBS? WHAT A STUPID WORLD WE LIVE IN! IF PEOPLE CAN'T EVEN UNDERSTAND THAT A GARBAGE COLLECTOR IS AS NECESSARY AS A STUPID BASKETBALL COACH IN AMERICA WHO EARNS 5,000,000 F-ING DOLLARS A YEAR, THEN WHAT THE HELL CAN THEY UNDERSTAND???

I just took a bath. I had to. When my mind starts running wild I jump in the tub. We have two bathrooms. One has a shower and one has a bathtub. When Daddy and I moved into the apartment he somehow started using the bathroom with the tub and I took over the one with the shower. I don't know why. Usually women like baths and men like showers. From what Marcel tells me, a large percentage of the male species use the shower as a place to rid themselves of the excess reproductive material that is produced daily in the pouch that dangles between their legs. Showers are much better than tubs in that the released 330,000,000 sperms cells curl cleanly down the drain and don't end up floating around in one's bath water. Ha!Ha! Maybe Daddy was past the age where...Hey, did you notice I said "We have two bathrooms"? What could be more beautiful than that. Daddy's been dead for eleven and a half months and he's still the other half of my "we". So he's not dead. Of course he's dead. But he's in my head all the time. He's in my head a lot more than 99.99% of people who are still alive. So is he alive? He's alive if I say so. I'm going to stop feeling sorry for myself for being an orphan. Mommy's alive too, but not as alive as Daddy because she died when I was eight and back then my brain only recorded a few things that have stuck around until today. Before Daddy died my brain recorded tons of junk that's stuck, like hearing Daddy's bath water run for five minutes before he set his body in the soap suds. He always had a bubble bath. He'd usually shave too after the bath. By then the door would be open and he'd have a towel around his waist and I could see the back of him when I walked past his bathroom. I never saw Daddy as a sexual object. I don't think he ever saw me as one either. I have a hunch that's the way it should be. Anyway, after Daddy went on full-time vacation in the stratosphere, I started taking the baths.

My paper. My paper on Hemingway for Mr. Fluckinger. I wrote it after my bath. The idea came to me in the tub. Have you ever wondered where ideas come from? Daddy and I used to talk about this all the time. Ideas just come. They don't come when "I" want them to come. "I" can't turn my brain on and off.

I actually had fun writing my paper. Like I said, my continued education isn't as crucial for me as it is for other kids. I can take a few chances with people like Mr.

Fluckinger. Instead of writing what I think he wants to hear, I can write what I want to say. Lucky me.

Here   it is:

Simple and Complex: Hemingway's World
By Laura Winger

Ernest Hemingway's book, "Farewell to Arms", almost sent me to the nuthouse. When Catherine and the baby die at the end, how can one remain sane? There are Catherines and babies who really do die in childbirth. How can one not go crazy in a world where such things happen? How? How? I didn't cry when I closed the book. I couldn't cry. The world was too cruel a place to cry in. The narrator leaves the hospital and walks home in Lausanne, in the dark, in the rain. The world is crying, not the narrator. Not me.

The subject for this paper is what is hidden behind the simplicity of Hemingway's writing style. I would have said what Marcel Monnet said...NOTHING...but since Marcel said it, I'll say something else. How do I know Marcel said that? Because I helped him correct his English. He's smart enough to ask me to help him. If you didn't want me to help him you shouldn't have given us a paper to write at home. I liked his paper very much. If I were you I would give him a top grade. But you probably won't.

Why am I talking to you – the teacher – like this? Because I just decided to be honest for once. Everybody is always saying how "honesty" is a value in our civilization. But that's the biggest lie in the world. People very rarely say what they "honestly" think. They say what they need to say under whatever circumstances they're in to get what they want. Everybody (people with so-called "brains") calculates everything that they say and when they say it. That is what they are "honest" about. They are honest about trying to get what they what. What comes out of their mouths isn't "honest"...it's calculated bullshit, bullshit warmed up in the brain, fried, cooled, refrigerated, then shit out all over the world. That's the way it has to be probably. Can you imagine a world in which people say what they honestly think? You...you...you, Mr. Fluckinger, a seemingly happily married husband, father of two, successful teacher, etc.... if you said what you honestly thought, you would walk down a busy street and every ten seconds you'd see a little cutie like me or my friend Natasha and say, "Gee baby, would I ever like to go to bed with you!"...or... "Holy shit! Look at the knockers on that babe!"... and you'd spend half your life getting slapped in the face. Or, if you and your fellow teachers told the truth to each other about what you really thought of each other, a war would probably break out in the teachers' room and everybody would start throwing coffee cups and chairs at each other.

But...so... just for once, I thought I would sit down and write what I really "honestly" thought... WITHOUT calculating what I needed to say to get a good "note" (as you call them here in beautiful Switzerland…and I really do think this country is beautiful. And you were lucky you were born here and not in the middle of the Sahara desert where your skinny ass would probably have died of starvation or malaria before the age of five. Actually, I don't know if you have a skinny ass. I've never seen your ass. But I'd like to. No I wouldn't. Yes I would. I'm not sure if I would. What would your wife say?)

So, I think Hemingway thought like I think…that the only way to keep from going crazy in this world is to become insensitive. It's as simple as that. There is so much horror going on at every second, so much killing, so many so-called "animals" eating and getting eaten, so many people dying of illness or accidents or simply of "old age", the only solution – the SIMPLE solution – is to block it all out, ignore it, not care about it.

The human head is not equipped to deal with the reality of life. It must simplify like Hemingway does with language.

There is one more thing I want to say before my two-page limit has expired. (And why a two-page limit, Mr. Fluckinger? I know why: so you don't have to correct too much bullshit. And you're right. You have other things to do I'm sure. Better things. No one should spend half a lifetime correcting papers.)

The one more thing I want to say is this: Usually people who write in a complicated style end up saying stupid simple stuff. They pretend like they are giving answers to questions that really have no answers because they are infinitely complicated. Take Immanuel Kant for example. (Too bad he wasn't named Kunt…he probably would have sold more books…Ha!Ha!) My dear old dead daddy explained to me – one nice warm spring day while we were driving through the Black Forest – that this guy Kant wrote a very windy complicated book called "A Critique of Pure Reason". In this book he ends up saying something very simple, ie that human beings always see things in a certain way because of the make-up of their heads and brains. You can't get out of your head. Daddy said Kant said that people CAN'T really KNOW ANYTHING because of this. But then he ends up saying HE KNOWS "THE TRUTH". (Was Kant a Kunt?) Daddy said this is the kind of thing most philosophers do. Hemingway is the opposite. He says simple things that hide the complexity of everything. At the end of "Farewell to Arms" you don't feel like there are solutions. No solutions implies complexity. Only feelings – like love – are simple. They are either there or they aren't. Existence is complicated. It is infinite and can't be understood. People try to understand it by simplifying it. But they're fooling themselves.

It's as simple as that.

4

I really do have a friend named Natasha. She is pretty much the only girl friend I like to hang out with for more than ten minutes. We became friends when Daddy died. All the kids in my class were real nice and all and came up to me and said how sorry they were and how they had had a grandfather or an uncle or a hamster that had died so they knew exactly how I felt. I know they all meant well and a few even cried real tears. But for whatever reason, deep down inside I had the feeling that they were kind of acting out a part in a play and didn't really care two cents about Daddy or me. But how could they have cared about Daddy in that Marcel Monnet is the only one who had ever met him. I probably would have done the same thing if one of their fathers had kicked the bucket...Anyway, Natasha was kind of refreshing in that she didn't get all sentimental, but one day just said, "So Laura, what are you going to do now?" It struck me as a really good question and kind of the only one that was relevant to anything. What was I going to do?...Even though I had had time to prepare for Daddy's death, I wasn't really ready for it. For a couple of weeks I was a zombie and thought the world was a giant cesspool and all that. But the fact was that I still had to do something. I guess I could have kept moping around for a few years and thinking deep existential thoughts about being alone in the universe, but I guess deep deep deep down inside I knew I still wanted to live a decent life. A couple of times I thought suicide might be an option, but I knew I didn't really have the guts or the desire to kill myself. And fortunately I didn't because today I'm quite used to being an orphan with my own apartment and freedom to do whatever the hell I want to do whenever the hell I want to do it. I realize now that people can basically get used to anything, including no parents. Look at Eskimos living in minus-forty-degree weather or Ethiopians living in plus-forty-degree weather! You can live with two parents or one parent or zero parents. People get used to tsunamis or world wars or earthquakes killing thousands. Laura Winger can get used to no Daddy. And like I said, he really isn't dead in that I think about him and talk to him all the time. I just don't have to do his dishes and watch saliva pop out of the corners of his mouth anymore…

Anyway, a few days after Daddy's funeral Natasha invited me to go to a nice restaurant down by the lake in Ouchy. I think her daddy's kind of rich and maybe he gave her the money, but she still had the idea to take me out to dinner. We went to the Café Beau Rivage and the food was delicious and actually made me forget about death for a while which I think was Natasha's goal in the first place. We ate and talked for three hours and got to know each other pretty well. Usually getting to know people turns out to be rather boring, but Natasha turned out to be really rather interesting. She is one of those

Europeans who has got ancestry from ninety different countries. Her mother's from Russia, her father's German, but his mother was Greek, and her mother's father was Polish etc...etc...all of which just makes me think how stupid "nationalities" are. When you think that in the history of the world, borders have changed about as often as people change underwear (there were probably no borders at all for a few billion years, back before people started wearing underwear) and so for a long time "nationalities" didn't even exist. Had you been born a hundred or a thousand years earlier you would have had a completely different name and would have spoken a completely different language. But we're so stupid we all say "I'm American" or "I'm Swiss" like it means something. I guess people need to feel they belong to a group or a club and think that theirs is the coolest...

Back to Natasha. When we were eating dinner, every subject that came up was easy to talk about. I guess, in the end, that's what friendship is. One thing that she and I really had in common was that we had read a lot of the same books. Of course people can read the same book, but see it completely differently, so in the end it's as if they had not read the same book at all. But in our case, it was like we had experienced things together. We had both read "Death in Venice", "The Grapes of Wrath", "Anna Karenina", and all kinds of stuff. It almost felt like we'd been around the world together.

The only big difference between us is that she comes from this devout religious "Orthodox" family, whatever "orthodox" means. She tried to explain it all to me, but I mix everything up. All I know is they have their own "Pope" and they think they've got the real truth and that the Catholics and the other pope screwed up somewhere along the line and they've only got part of the truth. We didn't talk about it, but as far as I know Natasha is still a virgin like her mommy and daddy want her to be, but I got the idea it was more because she hadn't met the right guy yet than because she was afraid of going to hell if she made love. I'm sure we'll have the conversation one day…the conversation about our bodies that are so smooth even street lamps turn their heads and check us out when we walk by LOL.

Anyway, Natasha and I are friends. And we became friends at a very good time for me.

5

I guess I'll probably keep going to school. With teachers like Mr. Fluckinger I'd be a fool to stop. I had him all wrong. I had called him a pedantic pinhead. I thought he'd hate my paper on Hemingway. It turns out he loved it. He even made a special appointment to talk to me one day after school. He said he had two choices: to turn me into the school authorities for sexual harassment or give me a top note. He gave me the top note. He said in fifteen years of teaching nobody had ever written a paper like that. He said that when he was a student he "didn't have the balls" to write a paper like that. He said it, not me. Why, when it comes to discussions of courage, are the expressions always about MALE anatomy? Even in French they say, "Il – ou elle - n'a pas des couilles". They don't say "Elle – ou il - n'a pas des nichons"… All right. Let's face it…men are pigs trying to dominate the stupid farm. Only some end up getting sent to the slaughterhouse… Poor them…Actually in the end we all go to slaughter…

I'm straying again. I stray all the time. My mind constantly jumps from one subject to another. Is that bad? Is it good? Is it because I had a ringside seat at the boxing match of life and got to watch my mother get knocked out in the second round by a vicious uppercut and my father slowly pummeled to the ground in a grueling eighth round? Maybe all human brains are "straying" all the time. Maybe some just have a longer leash. Why do some brains watch game shows and eat potato chips all day and others read Shakespeare and suck champagne? Does reading Shakespeare make a brain "better"? Maybe in Mr. Fluckinger's eyes it does...

Anyway, he, dear Mr. Fluckinger, wanted to talk to me. After he told me that he really did like my paper, I couldn't help wondering if he liked more about me than just my paper and that he had just used my paper as an excuse to be alone with me in his classroom after school and everything that goes along with all that. I even wondered if that's what I was hoping for all along. But the meeting was as innocent as a nun meeting a priest in a dentist's office. It went like this:

Laura, I guess you know what I want to talk to you about.

Sure, Mr. Fluckinger. My paper on Hemingway, right?
Exactly.
Well, do you think I'll be the next Bronte sister?
Maybe.
What do you mean? Don't tell me you liked it?
I really did like it, Laura. I really did. The truth is that your paper and your friend Marcel Monnet's paper were the only two papers that got top notes.
So you weren't mad that I corrected Marcel's paper.
Of course not. I'm not so stupid to think that when I give you a weekend to write something, you're not going to try

to get a little "outside" help. The goal of this paper was to try to get students to "think" a little and maybe learn a few new things in English along the way. I don't care if your parents or Oscar Wilde help you…

My parents and Oscar Wilde are all dead.

I know. You know what I mean.

Of course. So you didn't mind that I helped Marcel?

Yes… No, I didn't mind. The thing that mattered was that Marcel did some thinking and learned a little English. I think he did both. And you, you definitely did some thinking.

I can't help thinking…I can't turn the machine off.

Since your parents passed away…

They didn't "pass away" Mr. Fluckinger (we were having this conversation in English). They died…D-I-E-D. Died like all the other ninety-nine million trillion zillion dead creatures in the history of the planet earth.

I'm sorry…

Sorry for them or sorry for me? You can't be sorry for them. You didn't even know them.

Okay, for you.

Should you be sorry for me? Maybe I'm the luckiest kid in the world. Maybe my parents died at exactly the right time. Maybe if they had lived together for ten more minutes they would have started hating each other and fighting like hell and throwing wine glasses at each other, and I would have been the screwed-up kid who had to watch it all.

Maybe. Of course one never knows.

Did you know my mother died when I was eight?

No, I didn't know that.

There are a lot of things you don't know.

I never said the contrary.

I know you didn't. I'm just talking. I just think it's funny how teachers judge their students all the time and they don't really KNOW anything about the people they're judging. How can you judge somebody when you don't know EVERYTHING about the person? Only then can you judge somebody. And since nobody ever knows everything about anybody, nobody has the right to judge anybody.

I guess we judge people because we have to. We have to decide who gets to go to the university and who doesn't. There has to be limits.

My father used to tell me that the only thing that really stuck with him from his Christian upbringing was Jesus saying "Judge not that ye be not judged". He used to laugh because he said Christians today judge people like crazy. In fact, they're probably some of the most judgmental people on the planet. Daddy said there was only one true Christian and he died on the cross.

I would have liked to meet your father.

At this point in the conversation I started to get a little nervous because Mr. Fluckinger was saying all the right things and was letting me say whatever I wanted to say, which is something most people – including me – appreciate. I mean there aren't many people on earth to whom you can really say everything you want to. That was my point in my paper on Hemingway when I said nobody's really honest because you can't be honest in this world. Except maybe once or twice in a lifetime. I guess that's what's I loved so much about Daddy. He was really the one person I felt I could pretty much say anything and everything to. And now I started getting this feeling with Mr. Fluckinger and it scared me a little. I don't know exactly why, but it did. But I didn't get up and run out of the room or anything...

Yeah, he was a nice guy.

I imagine so when I see his daughter...

Which is to say he thought I was some kind of hot shit teenager. But the thing is, he didn't really make me feel like a teenager. He made me feel like me. I know it sounds kind of dumb, but that's the way Daddy was too. He always made me feel like me, not a dumb kid, or an adolescent, or whatever...just me.

So back to your paper, Laura... How did you think I'd respond when I read it?

I didn't really think about how you'd respond. I just wrote what I wanted to say. I wrote the whole thing in about thirty minutes. I just said what I wanted to say and hung up the phone...I mean clicked "PRINT" and turned off the computer...

And you didn't care what I would think?

Not then. Then I didn't care if I was writing to you, my dead grandmother, Hemingway himself, or the Holy Ghost. I just wrote what I wanted to say.

And that's what was so refreshing.

Thirty seconds of silence. He broke it.

Laura, what you said made sense.

Mr. Fluckinger, I'm not really sure if anything makes sense in this world anymore.

Maybe that's the first sign of intelligence.

My father is the one who got me to think about things.

What did he do?

He was a business professor here. But before he studied business he had studied philosophy.

That's a rare combination. He died when?

A little more than a year ago.

I suddenly saw Daddy. I mean really saw him. It's hard to explain. For a bunch of seconds Mr. Fluckinger became a blur. He disappeared. Daddy appeared. Daddy dead. Daddy alive. Mr. Fluckinger alive. Mr. Fluckinger dead. Daddy filling my eyes and head like my own blood and brain. Mr. Fluckinger melting into the wall behind him. I suddenly felt the separation between the dead and the living disappear…

Eventually Mr. Fluckinger came back into focus. We finished our conversation. He never showed any signs that he had the hots for me.

6

I met Johnny two days ago. I was on my way to the Mövenpick for an ice cream. He and this girl were walking a few meters in front of me. Suddenly the girl stopped and shouted, "Johnny, what's wrong with you?" He very calmly answered back, "Everything. Anything wrong with that?" Then she made a fist and smacked him on the arm and ran off down the street. He didn't move. I stopped. He started rubbing his arm though I doubt it really hurt. He sensed there was somebody behind him. He turned, half-smiled at me, and said, "Ah…love!" The only thing I could think of to say was, "Are you okay?" He pointed a long finger down the road and said, "She doesn't think so."

You must understand that since my boyfriend Chuck, I haven't had much going on in the way of a love life. When you've been out in the cold for a while, you kind of tend to look at everybody you meet (of the opposite sex that is…unless you're homo- or bi-sexual) as a potential person to light a fire with. You don't really do it on purpose, but that's just the way the brain works. If you're in love with somebody, other people aren't so important and they're kind of just like passing cars or clouds. But when you're alone or lonely, other people suddenly get your mental radar screen to start flashing THIS PERSON MIGHT BE SOMEBODY I COULD LIKE!

THIS PERSON MIGHT BREAK THE DROUGHT! ATTENTION! POTENTIAL BOYFRIEND! So, being the dumb-dumb I am, I started to get a little nervous and damp in the armpits, because Johnny was kind of cute and I figured anybody who admitted that everything was wrong with himself couldn't be a bad guy.

"I mean your arm," I said.

"I know you meant my arm," he said. "That's one advantage boys have over girls. When you hit us it usually doesn't hurt as much as when we hit you."

"Do you hit a lot of girls?"

"Not yet. But if she comes back…" He made a fist and smiled.

"You don't look like the girl-hitting type."

"It's never too late to get started."

I took a half of a step downhill closer to him. His girlfriend was out of sight. Suddenly I wondered if I'd rather get hit by a boy or a boy's girlfriend.

"Does she hit a lot?" I said.

"She watches too much TV."

"And you don't?"

"Not as much as she does. I think a thousand years from now people will look back at us and laugh their asses off about how we wasted our time on earth watching TV and movies."

"Maybe a thousand years from now TV will be worse."

"Good point."

"Maybe there's TV in heaven."

"I never thought of that."

"There could be anything in heaven. My father used to say if God made the earth, there was no guarantee he'd make a better heaven."

"Smart guy."

"He was."

Neither of us said anything for a moment. I watched his eyes drop to my feet and climb back up to my face.

"What's your name?"

"Laura."

"Laure or Laura?"

"Laura."

"I'm Johnny."

"I know."

"How do you know?"

"I heard your girlfriend say 'What's wrong with you, Johnny?' Aren't you going to go after her?"

"It's too late now. She likes to run away."

Gone with the Wind, I thought, but didn't say. Instead I said, "So how'd you get a name like Johnny here in Switzerland?" We were speaking French.

"My mother loved Johnny Hallyday. She still does. She always tries to drag us to his concerts because she always says 'This one might be his last.'"

"Do you go?"

"I went last summer in Geneva."

"How old is your mother?"

"Old enough to stop liking Johnny Hallyday. Fifty."

"I still like the Beatles."

"But you're not fifty."

"Why can't she like whatever she wants to like?"

"She can. Sometimes I just think she likes Johnny Hallyday more than anybody else including my father."

"I guess people like to dream."

"Reality is better."

"I guess so. If you can find good reality."

We each moved a step closer. There was about a meter between us now.

"So Johnny," I continued, "why did your girlfriend hit you?"

"Why do you think? You're a girl. You know better than I do."

"Because she doesn't like the way you comb your hair…"

"I stopped combing my hair when I was fifteen."

"Because she says you never listen to her…"

"I listen. I just don't like what I hear."

"Because you're a Moslem and she's a Hindu and she wishes you were reincarnated as Johnny Depp…"

"You're getting closer."

"Because she caught you staring at a beautiful fly on another girl's nose…except there was no fly."

"You're a genius. But I don't even remember the girl I was accused of staring at."

"Is that all that's wrong with you?"

"It depends on who you're asking."

Neither of us said anything for a few seconds. I sensed we both sensed that we were at that crucial moment where either we exchange some kind of contact information – last name, email, phone number… anything to keep the other alive – or we go our separate ways and leave another meeting to chance. But why let randomness rule when you can control part of your destiny?

"Where do you live?" he said before I said anything.

"Up the street, on the Boulevard de Grancy. And you?"

"Avenue de France."

"With her?" I figured I had nothing to lose.

"Sometimes."

"And you?"

"I live alone."

"Where's the rest of your family? You're not Swiss, are you? You don't have much of an accent, but you don't sound Swiss."

"I'm not. I was born in America, in California, but my father and I moved here when I was ten."

He didn't ask about my mother so I told him.

"My mother died when I was eight. They had me late."

"No brothers and sisters?"

"Zero."

"When did your father die?"

"A little over a year ago. I like it here. I can't see any reason to go anywhere else right now."

"Are you in school."

"At the gymnase… Auguste Piccard. What about you? Do you go to school?" I figured he was a few years older than I am.

"No. I stopped. I dropped out of law school. I hated it. I work in the post office at night sorting mail. Somebody has to do it. I have no idea what I want to do when I grow up. I guess I hope I never grow up. My father's a lawyer and his father's a lawyer and he wanted me to take over the family business. I couldn't do it."

"Why not?"

"I guess I don't care enough about the law."

Suddenly Johnny just looked at me, but I got the feeling he was looking more inside himself than at me. That happens a lot with people. They stare at you, but they're really staring at themselves. His eyes got kind of narrow and his mouth started moving but he didn't say anything. Suddenly he pulled his phone out of his pocket. "Could I have your number?"

I gave it to him.

"Listen, it was nice meeting you, but I'd better be going," he said.

And he went.

7

I don't think most students realize how lucky they are to be in "school". I put school in quotation marks, because it's really more like a fun park. I mean, where else can you see 500 kids your own age every day. It really reminds me of Monkey Island in the San Francisco Zoo. Daddy used to take me there before we moved to Switzerland. The zoo is right next to the ocean and we always had to wear a jacket, even in summer. The only thing I really remember was this big reddish concrete island full of what looked like the happiest monkeys in the world. They would all hop around, swing from branch to branch, laugh at each other, scratch under their arms and on the tops of their heads, and every now and then stop to nibble on a piece of carrot or banana or something. They always had food and friends. There must have been about a hundred of them. They didn't have to work. They didn't have to hunt or shop for food. They didn't have to sweep up their messes or clean their toilets…That's kind of the way school is: a few hundred monkeys in the same building; food in the cafeteria; cleaners vacuuming, mopping the floors, and cleaning the bathrooms; recesses where the monkeys get to babble and squawk; lots of members of the opposite sex running around keeping everyone excited… Paradise! Monkey Island! The gymnase of Auguste Piccard!

I guess the only real difference between us and the monkeys is that the monkeys don't have "teachers" and they don't have to sit on hard wooden chairs for five or six hours a day and keep their mouths shut. When I was younger, in the "college", I used to get bored to death, but now I've turned over a new leaf. Since Daddy died, I've made a conscious decision to try to never waste time. Even if the teacher is the most soporific lame-brain in the universe, I have decided to never be bored because I can always let my brain do the talking. I'm there, in my chair, happy, healthy, alive, not ugly, food in my stomach, clothes to keep me warm ...and I can think about whatever I want in the whole wide human universe! Nowhere is it written that you have to listen to a teacher. Of course you're supposed to, but you don't have to. I always start by listening for a while, but then, more often that not, I start "talking to myself". I think, analyze, question, wonder if any of what the teacher is saying has anything to do with any part of me or if any part of me thinks any part of this can be of any use to anybody on earth. One question I often ask myself is, "Of all the things in the universe that this teacher could be saying, why is he or she saying what (s)he's saying???" Sometimes I dream. Sometimes I tell myself stories. But I've decided life is too short to let myself get bored...

Take this morning for example. (I should be doing homework, but it's much more fun to write my book!) My history teacher, Mr. Fleury (short, kind of fat, quite funny), was talking about the great Renaissance men like da Vinci and Michelangelo and how they knew so much about so many things. First I thought about Daddy and how he had two university degrees but knew absolutely nothing about how to fix a car or a toilet or how electricity worked. Then I wondered why nobody ever talks about Renaissance women or Renaissance goats, always just Renaissance men. Then I started thinking that probably 99% of all Americans who study the Renaissance don't know what the word "renaissance" means or where it comes from because they've never studied French or Latin. Since it means "re-born", I started thinking about re-born Christians in America and how they all seem to be perfectly happy about who they are re-born into and never seem to imagine the possibility that since they were re-born once, they might be re-re-born and re-re-re-born and in their next life might end up believing in Hinduism where everything and everybody plays musical chairs all the time and gets re-born into termites or Elvis Presley…Then my mind got all excited about how it's much more difficult to be a Renaissance man today than it was five hundred years ago because there's so much more to know today than there was to know five hundred years ago. Just take the subject of "history", for example. Da Vinci and Michelangelo only had to learn everything that happened up in the world up to the year 1550. Today if you want to be a Renaissance kind of guy (or gal or goose or goat) you not only have to learn everything that happened up to 1550, but you also have to learn everything that has happened from 1550 to 2012! That's 462 more years to know everything about everything, which includes the French Revolution, the slave trade, Mozart, Beethoven, the Beatles, the American Revolution, the Civil War, Two World Wars, Vietnam, a trip to the moon, Iraq, Afghanistan, Marilyn Monroe, Bruce Willis, Walt Disney, Mickey Mouse, cars, telephones, Gustave Flaubert, Proust, nuclear physics, Hugh Hefner, Heisenberg, Henry Ford, etc…etc…and I haven't even mentioned anything about China, Indonesia, Switzerland, Senegal, South America, Singapore, Somalia, Iceland, Canada, or the millions and millions of people who weren't part on any of the above topics, but who were born and died and are still part of "history". It is pretty funny to think that when you study "history" people always pick out the same topics over and over again. It's also funny to think that there were probably a few zillion years of "history" before "History" started to be written about or studied…and on and on…And that's just the subject of history. Imagine what has gone on in the last 500 years in astronomy, chemistry, philosophy, medicine, biology, anthropology, music, and literature! There are so many books about so many things that if you studied all day for eighty years you probably couldn't read one-thousandth of them. Leonardo and Michelangelo probably didn't have more than fifteen books in their whole library!

Anyway, you get the point. Mr. Fleury didn't have a chance to bore me. No matter who's babbling in front of the class, there's always something to think about. Actually sometimes boring stuff stimulates me more than interesting stuff. It often gets me thinking about how most people are so full of crap that they must spend three-fourths of their lives on the toilet! But hey, it's fun to think that it's impossible to know everything about anything, much less anything about everything. The world keeps turning and teachers keep talking. If I really think about it…if I really get up on my toes and scrub the ceiling of my brain…the idea of a Renaissance man is as much bullshit as anything else. History books invented the Renaissance man. Da Vinci and Co. knew a few things about a few subjects, but there were a zillion other things they didn't know one single solitary iota about…like the stupid fact there were no "Indians" in America, because Columbus didn't find India, but rather Cuba or Florida or wherever the hell he was! (When I think that Americans still call the Sioux and Apache "Indians" and that these fine people still live on places called "reservations", I want to vomit all over my "history" book!)

I often wonder if Susan and William Winger would have wanted their daughter Laura to go to "THE UNIVERSITY". I just realized – when I saw it in capital letters - that the word "university" has the word "universe" in it. One would think that if one went to the university the first thing one would study would be "THE UNIVERSE" to maybe get a little perspective on the whole mess. But that's obviously not the case…Back to

Mommy and Daddy. Daddy probably would have said, "Laura darling, life is short. Do what you want to do without screwing up the world or other people." The fact that Daddy and I never talked much about my future education before he died says everything. As for Mommy, I didn't get to know her well enough to know what she thought about much of anything, except how to make pancakes and how Winnie-the-Pooh was really a nice bear that could talk and think just like humans. But my guess is that since she and Daddy agreed on a lot of stuff (which is probably why they got along pretty well), she probably would have said the same thing as Daddy. At least that's the impression Daddy gave me when I asked him about their relationship before he was in too much pain or too drugged up to talk about anything anymore.

One of the last things Daddy used to joke about was how people at "the university" always act like what they're saying is "true". Of course some teachers are smart enough to know that there will be a new version of "the truth" in a hundred years or a thousand years, or a hundred days, or even ten minutes…but most professors act like they "know" the truth. Daddy used to laugh about how people – teachers or anybody else for that matter – say "I know" all the time…I know this and I know that. Daddy would say, "What can a person really know? Maybe you can know how to build a bridge or a bomb, but can you know if the bridge and the bomb are good or bad for the world? You can know how to make a cheeseburger, but can you know if cheeseburgers are good and bad for the world? They're certainly bad for the cow. You can know what the score of the baseball game is, but can you ever know the hearts and minds of the players and whether or not baseball is a stupid waste of time on this earth?" You see, Daddy taught ethics… business ethics. Some of my friends say that all business is unethical. Daddy used to say that all ethics were unethical. He thought it was impossible to know what was good or bad or right or wrong. What's good for one person can be bad for another. People always think what's right and wrong for themselves should be right and wrong for everybody else. (Who first invented this idea?) But they never think about the fact that probably no two people on earth exactly agree on what's right and wrong about everything. Daddy used to say that nobody thought about the problem of morality itself. That was the real problem! One day when he was still in the mood for talking, we had a conversation that wasn't really a conversation because he did all the talking. But I didn't mind because I knew he wouldn't be around much longer. I'll never forget it because he talked like he was a little delirious, but he seemed as lucid as a light bulb. It went something like this:

Who is to say if getting married is good or bad? Who's to say if Bush messed up in Iraq? Maybe Iraq will be a cool place one day with great golf courses and five-star hotels. Are five-star hotels "good"? Is golf "good"? Maybe golf is good for marriage? Maybe the wife is happy because golf keeps the husband away and while he's away she can sneak off and do what she wants…like see her lover or buy extra absolutely totally unnecessary clothes that are absolutely NECESSARY for her. Maybe the lover keeps the marriage together. Maybe the lover is bad for the marriage because infidelity is supposed to be immoral. Maybe fidelity is immoral. Maybe golf is good for marriage but bad for the environment. But what is the "environment"? Aren't people part of the environment? Golf makes people happy. It keeps them out of trouble. It keeps them out of their spouses' hair. What about Afghanistan? A big mistake? A moral war? Talibans are not like termites. They're much harder to exterminate. Harder than Saddam Hussein. But they want to exterminate us…so who is right? On what grounds? Whose Bible is right? And what if they're all wrong? Obama said he'd close Guantanamo right after getting elected. He didn't. Was he right or wrong? Don't ask Al Qaida. Maybe in 2035 there will be great ski resorts in Afghanistan. After a nice day on the slopes Afghans will be able to sip a glass of white wine in a cosy chalet with a fire in the fireplace like they do in Switzerland. Maybe they'll even have the Winter Olympics in Kabul and a Taliban woman will carry the torch. Will she wear the veil? But skiing wrecks the environment too. Are skiers part of the environment? Of course not, most people say. Of course they are, I say. How can people be part of the environment? people say. How can people not be part of the environment? I say…

I remember Daddy was like a volcano that day. He was talking so fast that saliva balls were popping out of both corners of his mouth (normally they'd just come out of the left side, left from his perspective). And now the volcano is silent. My one and only Daddy. Dead. But like I said, Daddy's not really dead because I still talk to him all the time. We still talk for hours and hours, just like we used to do at the dinner table or in the car when we'd go on little weekend trips to the Black Forest or Alsace or Zermatt. (That's what's so wonderful about Switzerland. In a couple of hours you can be in so many great places.) I think good and evil might have been Daddy's favorite subject. He loved to see how the good and the bad changed depending on who was talking. People would accuse him of "moral relativism". And he would answer, "Do you know what's right or wrong? No, you don't. Nobody does. It's not moral relativism; it's thinking and admitting the limits of the human head."

That was Daddy. People didn't like to hear that, of course. People want meat and potatoes. People want Gods with capital "G"s and Commandments with capital "C"s. They want prophets and prison cells and afterlives and Bibles to tell them who's right and who's wrong. They want to cheer for the "Home team", the team in the blue and white uniform. Viva Italia! Vive la France! Viva l'España! (Spain just won the European football tournament! People honked their horns up and down the Boulevard de Grancy until one o'clock in the morning!) Daddy used to love this stuff. He said it reminded him of anthills or flocks of birds. He didn't think people were God's children; if anything they were cousins of grass, flowers, porcupines and penguins. He didn't believe in separating man from nature. He didn't believe in free will. He thought people were no different than the rest of existence. They were part of everything, part of "the environment". He loved to watch herds of anything. Cows, sheep, ducks, sports fans. Daddy didn't believe in chance or destiny. He just believed everything is…even guns in the ghetto or clouds in the sky…Everything is part of the great ocean of existence. Daddy saw no God setting it in motion or aiming it in any direction. No heaven or hell. No Renaissance man can possibly understand it all. The world wasn't made to fit into the human mind. Nowhere is it written that the universe is to be understood…you can study at the UNIVERSITY forever and ever and never understand the UNIVERSE! You can build the biggest telescopes and atom crushers in the world, you can read Freud and Jung until you're blind, you can sit in the library and study Plato and Einstein until your underpants turn green, but you still won't see into the human heart, you still won't understand the mystery of a flower, you still won't know how a chicken got to be a chicken, and you still won't know why one Daddy thinks this way and another Daddy thinks that way, and my Daddy thought everybody was crazy, including himself…

O Daddy, Daddy. Did you make me crazy? I'm not crazy. You're not crazy. Life is crazy.

It's almost midnight.

I must lay my body down.

Good body.
Smooth like a fish.
Thank you life, for making my body.
French test tomorrow.
English with Fluckinger.
Another day on Monkey Island.
Maybe Johnny will call.
I might need you Johnny.
O Johnny, Johnny…

8

Johnny didn't call. Not the next day or the next day or the day after that. He probably made up with his little pugilist cutie pie. He's probably a sado-masochist who likes getting punched by his girlfriend every so often to keep the relationship exciting. He probably forgot my name two minutes after we said goodbye. He's probably got a phone full of names and numbers of girls he's met on sidewalks and in cafés.

Bye Johnny. I can live without you. I lived without you for eighteen years. I can live without you for eighty more. Besides, maybe you have bad breath and stink when you sweat...

Forget Johnny... Let's talk about Chuck... Chuckie-the-Mormon... my boyfriend after Cherif. I was thinking about him this morning in French class while Mr. Shurter was talking about Madame Bovary. Don't get me wrong. I think Madame Bovary's a great book. But Emma's husband reminded me of Chuck. And I started thinking about how Chuck and I met and how we broke up. It's a nice story: girl meets boy in the grocery store.

Chuck was three years older than me (he still is for that matter). He was working a summer job as a cashier in the COOP supermarket across the street from where I live. It was about three months before Daddy died, just at the time when Daddy was starting to really fade off

54

the world's radar screen. I needed somebody to talk to…to talk to about Daddy and to talk to period because after his tirade about good and evil, Daddy didn't talk much. I used to always go to Chuck's check-out line to pay for my stuff. It was obvious he thought I was cute and I thought he was cute. Being cute is at least a start in this world. Anyway, one day I told him I lived just across the street and one thing led to another and the next thing I knew he had kind of invited himself over for a drink after he finished work at seven. A drink for Chuck was lemonade or Coke because his religion says alcohol, tea, and coffee are all evil and if you drink them your rosy rear-end will end up getting barbecued in hell. Actually he wasn't even supposed to drink Coke because it has caffeine in it and his Mormon Bible says caffeine is a sin. When I asked him why God put caffeine on the earth if it was a sin, he said man needed temptations to prove his worthiness to go to heaven. Chuck's religion has an answer for everything. I guess all religions do.

Anyway, Chuck said he could drink Coke because it had just a little caffeine and a little caffeine was all right with God and the eternal rules of the universe. Well, it turns out the same thing was true about me…a little Laura Jezabel Winger was all right, but a lot was a sin! Chuck could hold my hand, kiss my lips, and slightly (sort of un…un…in…tentionally) brush his fingers across my beautiful breasts when we were kissing or fooling around on the bed, but that was ALL. The rest of me was…A SIN! NO TOUCHING BARE BOOBS! NO

HANDS BETWEEN THIGHS! NO FINGERS PLAYING THE SINGLE KEY PIANO!…And the funny thing was, NO TOUCHING CHUCKIE'S FLAGPOLE EVEN IF IT WAS AT HALF-MAST! All that stuff was ONLY WHEN CHUCKIE AND I GOT MARRIED!!!…So to make a short story shorter, Chuck and I did a lot of kissing for a couple of months and during that time I came pretty close to talking him out of his religion. But, in the end, his religion won. It usually does. My flesh or him getting his flute played weren't worth the risk of going to hell. I didn't really mind losing. His version of heaven didn't sound like a whole lot of fun…

So – to continue the exciting history of my sexual education – up to this point in my eighteen years in this wonderful world of joy, sorrow, and annual dental appointments, I've been intimate with exactly three boys: Marcel Monnet, Cherif (funny, I can't even remember his last name… it was African… they're harder to remember than English or French names), and Chuckie Snyder. I often ask myself if any of what we experienced will stick with me or influence my relationship with my next boyfriend. My guess is that all these three have done is get me ready for a bone with a little more meat on it. Marcel was just a first dip in the water. But, since I didn't love him, I didn't want to swim for very long. Swimming with Cherif was fun, but after a while talking to him wasn't. Chuckie was another bag of potato chips. We never made love and we never really talked about anything interesting – except his most interesting religion. I guess what I'm trying to say is that I haven't hit love's jackpot yet. I wonder how many people really do. I guess at least I'm starting to know what love isn't…

The truth is, tonight I'm about as melancholy as I've been since Daddy died. Everything is kind of in slow motion. I'm lonely. I'm writing slowly. I'm thinking slowly. Usually my brain is like popcorn on a hot stove. Tonight it feels like it's had a novocaine shot. I can almost feel the earth turning. I wonder if it will stop one day and die like my love for Cherif did. Like everything else does? Boom! Motor broken. Car stops. Silence. Game over. Dead earth. Nowhere to fall, except into the sun. Flooommm! Sucked up. Sucked in. The start of a new black hole. What a world! Does the earth make noise as it flies through space? Airplanes do. Birds don't. Does it depend on who's listening? Or who has a motor? Birds don't have motors. Earths don't either. So what keeps birds and earths going? What keeps anything going? Cars die. Stars die. People die. Birds die. Plants die. Do rocks die?

What's wrong with me? At least my brain has started up again… Vroom! Vroom! … That's why I need Daddy. He'd say nothing is wrong with me. And he'd think with me. Think next to me. Daddy was company. A friend. Does anybody else think about these kinds of questions? Of course a few do. They're out there…somewhere in space… Do only people care about this kind of stuff? Do birds care? Do stars care? Do monkeys care? Do flies care? Of course not. So much the better for them. It makes life easy. Like Chuckie's religion. All the questions are answered. Nothing is a fuzz for the good God-fearing Mormons… or the full-blooded Pope-loving Catholics… or the flag-burning left-wingers who believe in justice and equality…or the idiots in class who believe in Renaissance men and a world "history" that is linear and nice and cute and clear-cut and "true"!!!…But I'm an idiot, too! Do you know why? Because asking all these "Winger" questions and "knowing" we don't know and "knowing" the world is probably just another wild animal floating in infinite space etc…"knowing" all this doesn't change anything about being in the world. You still have to live. You still have to get up in the morning. You still have to take the garbage out. You still have to eat. You still have to do something with those hormones popping off in your body. All the beauty and all the shit will still be there. The Renaissance men didn't know the earth was turning. But they knew other things. They had their own beauty and their own shit. They knew men would fly one day. They knew the body was a complicated miracle…So everybody has to live with their time, their world, what they are and what they have. If Chuckie thinks he's going to heaven, good for Chuckie. If Daddy didn't believe in truth and salvation, good for Daddy. If Mr. Fluckinger thinks I'm smart, thank you Mr. Fluckinger. If Johnny doesn't call, screw you Johnny - there are seven billion other fish in the damn ocean!

That's it… That's enough… Laura Winger is going to bed… in her empty apartment… It's not empty… it's full

of memories and all kinds of shit… Goodnight world…
Goodnight universe… Goodnight brain …………………

9

You know what I like about Laura Jezabel Winger? She always bounces back. She gets floored, but she gets up. She's a fighter. She doesn't get knocked-out easily. A mommy's death might drop her to her knees. But she'll get back on her feet. No more daddy…No problem, girl. Life goes on. There are worse things in this world than being an orphan. She could have been one of those kids from Belgium on that bus that crashed head-on into a wall in the tunnel in Sierre a couple of months ago. Happy, sun-stained faces, coming home from a school ski trip in the lovely village of St. Luc, Switzerland. Mommies and Daddies waiting for their dear cherubs (I loved that word from the moment I saw it) back home in Belgium. An hour on the road and boom! Head on at a 100 kilometers/hour straight into a cement wall. Everybody sitting in front died. Twenty-eight of them. Four teachers and twenty-four kids. They won't be getting up and fighting anymore. But their families and friends will. Just like Laura Jezabel. But she's not special. They're not special. The truth is that every damn creature on earth is in the boxing match of life. Everybody gets knocked down and scrambles back up for more…more slaps in the face, more punches to the gut, more rotten teeth, more thrills, more spills, more pain, more death…

But it's not all bad. There are prizes. There are moments. There are winners. There are good days. There are walks in the forest and afternoons at the beach. There are friends…

My friend Natasha is in the garbage these days. She didn't pass her school year and her mother found drugs in her school bag. They fought. She got back up. Her parents got back up. They go on…

If there is one thing I hate in this world, it is people who say "EVERYTHING HAPPENS FOR A REASON!" If I hear that one more time I'm going to throw up. Twenty-eight innocent people die in the blink of an eye in a smashed bus and the idiots say, "It happened for a reason." Hell yes, it happened for a reason…Either the bus driver fucked up or the bus fucked up…but that's not what the it-happened-for-a-reason people are talking about. No, no. They're talking about God, nice big God who is watching over the whole show and making sure everything happens exactly the way it's supposed to. It's God's universe. Everything makes sense in God's universe. Millions starve to death in Africa…just what God wanted! A Tsunami kills 220,000 people…God needed them upstairs to wash windows! Adolph is nuts and gasses six million…God has His reasons! Mother gets eaten by cancer…hey, maybe God needed her to wash dishes in heaven! Mothers die at childbirth…for a reason! Babies die at childbirth…for a reason! For what reason? I'll tell you for what reason…So people with pathetic lives can feel that their pathetic lives have a meaning. That's the reason! The real reason!

Why am I talking about this? Because I'm eighteen years old. Because I have to make sense of the circus. One way or another I have to put the puzzle together and keep my brain from exploding…

One good thing was that Daddy taught me not to be bitter. Daddy taught me not to blame anybody. He taught me that people can't be other than what they are. Nobody wants to be an idiot. Nobody wants to be an asshole. Nobody wants to see the world like a five-year-old. Thanks Daddy. You help me bounce back. People don't ask for the brains they have. Nothing in this universe asked to be what it is, the universe included.

I think it's time for me to say a prayer. I haven't said a prayer for a long time. It's not just people who believe in God and Jesus and the Virgin Mary who should get to say prayers. I'm going to pray to Daddy, my one and only daddy:

O dead Daddy mingling with the stars, hallowed be thy name. Please let us pray that nothing will be different because nothing can be different. Let us accept the entire bag of potato chips because what is IS. Nothing can be or should be different. This is what you tried to teach me. I was slow to learn, but now I think I feel it. Even if there are actual gods out there, they too are just part of what is. They too can be no different from what they are! Like all joy and suffering, all life and death, all clouds and blue sky, all mice and eagles, all mountains and valleys, all men who believe and disbelieve. Nothing can be other than what it is.

Nothing. People have been praying for thousands of years (and what is a thousand years to infinity? – nothing but a tiny puff of smoke), praying to every god under the sun…And what do we get? What does the world get?…The same old crap…Wars, murders, disease, starvation, bus crashes, dead kids, dead foxes, Hindus, Buddhists, Christians, atheists, Mormons, democrats, republicans, Obama, Romney, Assad, Putin…We are not saying that nothing will change because everything changes. But things will only change the way they can change and no other way. This is the world you described Daddy. Thank you dearest dead Daddy who gave me life and whose Daddy and Daddy and Daddy gave him life. And thank you Mommy and all Mommies of whom I might be a part one day in the great chain of life. Amen for now. But I'll be back.

I pray to Daddy because I never thought he was crazy and he never thought I was crazy. I keep him alive for both of us. Good night Daddy.

10

It's Monday morning, the end of June, 2012. School finishes on Friday. I'm up early. Showered. Dressed. Mr. Fluckinger wants to talk to me again after school today. I like talking to Mr. Fluckinger. It's not hard to understand why. He's a man, he likes me, he thinks I'm smart. I think he's smart. Last Thursday he stopped teaching his normal stuff with fifteen minutes left in the period. He passed out a clean piece of paper to everybody and said he was going to do something he had never done before in his teaching career. "All right everybody," he said with his deep voice that usually gets our attention, "listen carefully. Take out a pen. When I say 'GO' I want you to write NON-STOP ENGLISH until the bell rings. I want to see how many intelligible words you can put down on paper in exactly twelve minutes. It doesn't matter if you make mistakes. I just want your beautiful minds THINKING IN ENGLISH AND ONLY ENGLISH FOR TWELVE FULL MINUTES. That's not too much to ask. And I will give a top grade – "6" – to everybody who 'plays the game', who doesn't stop writing, and writes words that are part of the English language. This will be your last grade of the year."

This is why I like Mr. Fluckinger. No other teacher would dare do this kind of thing. No other teacher probably has the brains to do this kind of thing. Here's what I wrote. He gave it back to me on Friday. When you read it, you'll understand why he wants to talk to me:

English is a nice language with lots of words and syllables that make noise and you can say things like screw you Johnny saying you'd call and you don't it's bad enough having your goddamndaddykickthebucket and then your birds die and then to meet someone that you might really like that might fill up some of the holes in your body and mind and he says he'll call and doesn't so you think that maybe something's wrong with you but it's probably just the world but you should also think that it's just as possible that something is wrong with Johnny and he did say the first time you saw him that everything was wrong with him which you liked because nobody says that kind of thing. It's kind of the kind of thing Mr. Fluckinger might say himself or might have said when he was young and sexy but he's still young and sexy but I'm not trying to seduce him with this it's just what's coming out without thinking which is the whole idea of the twelve minutes non-stop writing and I won't erase anything or cross anything out because I like saying what I think once I a while. And now I'm thinking of what Mr. Fluckinger's nest is like at home and his wife and two kids and wishing sometimes that I'm a bird that could fly away where there is someone to truly love and somebody who truly loves me because love seems to be the goal of life but it's really not because it dies dead but maybe it doesn't and

That was twelve minutes of non-stop writing. Writing takes time. Especially with a pen and paper. I'll be back tonight with what happened with Mr. Fluckinger.

Back. He was in rare form today in class. He should have been an actor. Maybe he saw teaching as the next best thing…Anyway, we're finishing Steinbeck's "Of Mice and Men". We're not reading it for a test, but just "for the pleasure of reading." That's Mr. Fluckinger's whole thing…he wants us to read because WE want to read, not because HE wants us to read. Sometimes he acts out a scene for the class. Today it was when Curley's lonely desperate sexy wife seduces big crazy stupid sensitive Lenny in the barn before he – Lenny – accidentally kills her. Mr. Fluckinger acted both parts. He was a fat babbling Brad Pitt and Angelina Jolie rolled into one.

After the bell rang I waited until all the other kids had left and then I strutted to his desk kind of imitating his imitation of Curley's wife when she struts into the barn where Lenny is. I suddenly felt the amazing power a woman can have over a man. I sensed Mr. Fluckinger's eyes – eyes that were attached to his whole body – trying not to look at me, but looking at me. For a few seconds I had him. In those seconds I thought that there are probably very few attractions in the universe that are stronger than man for woman and vice-versa. Of course not any man for any woman or any woman for any man… but when the attraction is there, the eyes are like lightning bolts digging into the earth.

He actually laughed a little at my imitation and gestured for me to sit down at the desk nearest to his.

Good book, isn't it?

It's a great book, Mr. Fluckinger.

I'm glad you like it. Good imitation.

Thanks. You were especially good doing Curley's wife.

Try to see the film some day. The scene is very well done. We won't have time to see it together before the end of the year.

I will.

So you remembered I wanted to talk to you.

I have a pretty good memory.

I don't doubt it. I want to talk to you about a couple of things…

(Pause)

Laura, you're in a rather unique situation. I think you're the first student I've ever had who has lost both parents and who lives alone – independently – in the old family apartment. I just wondered how you are getting along.

If you want to know the truth, I'm starting to get used to it. At first it wasn't easy. But now – after more than a year – sometimes it's almost an exhilarating feeling to have absolutely no one looking over my shoulder telling me what to do and what not to do.

Not everybody could appreciate such freedom. Or make good use of it.

I know. I think about that every day. I think how

*unlucky I am, yet at the same time how lucky I might be…
at least I had parents that I loved and who loved me. Not
every kid can say that. Now I've got a life I can live however
I want to live it. Hardly any kid can say that.*

True.

*Not only that, but I was raised with essentially no idea
about what the "purpose" of life is. My parents did not
believe in any religion whatsoever and my father – who
taught business ethics – thought the whole moral history of
the world was one big messy bowl of soup.*

His words or yours?

*Mine I guess. But you get the point. I think you and my
father might have had a lot to talk about.*

I guess we'll never know.

*No…When I think about it, Daddy really taught me
three things: to be thankful I'm alive, to respect other
people and life in general, and to realize that things are
always much more complicated than they appear.*

*And all of that puts you in a very unique situation,
Laura. Most kids are either trying to please their parents
or are fighting against the principles that their parents
have taught them. You're doing neither.*

I know.

*At your age – eighteen, right? – to have no family
constraints, no religious constraints, and a very vague set
of rules as to what is moral and immoral is a very rare
situation indeed.*

At this point, I have to admit that I wondered what
Mr. Fluckinger was up to. He was talking about how free

I was and how I didn't have ninety million commandments nailed to my bedroom wall telling me how to live. I couldn't help thinking, "Is he just feeling me out to see if I might be free for…him?" I've seen enough movies and read enough books. I decided to turn the conversational steering wheel a little…

Didn't you want to talk to me about that twelve-minute paper we wrote last week?

Yes, I did. That was the other thing…What struck me, Laura – and I'll be honest with you – is that when I was reading your paper, I felt rather like I was your "father". I don't mean your "father" father. Of course not. I mean it seemed like you needed somebody to talk to…about your life…about this "Johnny", whoever he is, and it doesn't matter who he is… and I have to admit that I suddenly saw you as kind of a "daughter".

You have a daughter, don't you?

No, I have two boys.

Oh…

What I mean is, I'm sure your father was somebody you could really talk to. He's gone and…

Actually I still talk to him all the time.

I guess what I want you to know, Laura, is that you can feel free to talk to me any time if you need somebody to talk to. Given your situation, I thought I should tell you this as openly and clearly as possible. If you need anything, please feel free to ask. My wife and I would be most happy to help.

I have to admit, I liked hearing that "My wife and I". Even though Mr. Fluckinger is attractive and all, I am his student, and as far as I know, students aren't supposed to get into any hanky-panky with their teachers. The "My wife and I" just made that chair I was sitting in feel a little more comfortable.

That's nice of you Mr. Fluckinger. I really appreciate it.

It's the least I can do under the circumstances.

Under what circumstances? Does that mean "Because I'm your teacher and a married man, I can't fall in love with you and take you to Tahiti with me on a slow sailboat"? I can't help myself. I've read too many books…

I would suggest however, Laura, that you don't write things like you did last Thursday for your other teachers in other classes. You need to be careful about who you're talking to.

I know that Mr. Fluckinger. No, I wouldn't do that. I just thought you were the kind of person I could pretty much say anything to. I was just having fun. Talking to you is fun…

Well good…Just be careful. There's a difference between the public forum and the private forum.

Yeah, like on Facebook where you can send open messages and private messages.

I wouldn't know. I don't use Facebook.

I don't either really… No, don't worry, I'll try to be careful about who I'm talking to.

So we understand each other Laura.

Pretty much, I'd say.

Okay, just a few more days of school. What are your plans for the summer?

I have absolutely no plans. I haven't thought about it for two seconds.

That's not a bad way to live.

What about you Mr. Fluckinger?

We're going to Disneyland Paris and for a few days. The boys are at the right age...six and nine. Of course we'll spend some time in the city, too.

My father took me to the Disneyland in Los Angeles right after my mother died. I absolutely loved it. I still remember all the rides and stuff. I was eight...

Well, I hope my kids enjoy it. Actually, I've always wanted to see what it's like.

It's hard not to like it...no matter who you are.

We'll see.

He stood up. I stood up.

So thanks Laura.

Thank you Mr. Fluckinger.

11

Tuesday night. I got two phone calls this evening. First Mr. Fluckinger. Then Johnny. It was seven-thirty. I was watching the news. You know, I'm starting to hate the news. All news. TV, newspaper, radio, all the crap I get on the internet. It's such trash. But you don't care what I think about the news. You want to know about Mr. Fluckinger and Johnny. Probably mostly about Johnny because that's where you think the action might be. People want action. That's why there's all the crap in the news. It's all action. No substance. Just action. So here's Laura Jezabel Winger's action…

After I left Mr. Fluckinger's class yesterday afternoon and was moseying on home (I rarely walk fast – life is too short to hurry through it…haha!) I started thinking about a few things. I wondered if Mr. Fluckinger really did want to ask me about Johnny, but didn't dare. I wondered if he would have wanted to know about Johnny like a normal father would want to know about Johnny or if he would have wanted to know about Johnny like somebody who was interested in me would want to know about Johnny…

And also, Laura, I couldn't help but be a little concerned about the "Johnny" guy you wrote about in your text on Thursday. You've had enough disappointments in your life. I hope you're not involved in any complicated love stories.

Hey, I appreciate your concern, Mr. Fluckinger, but it's really no big deal at all. I was just thinking about this Johnny guy I met for about five minutes who took my number and said he'd call me and he hasn't. It's absolutely nothing to be concerned about.

I was just a little worried, that's all.

Don't worry, Mr. Fluckinger, I've read enough Jane Eyre and Anna Karenina to know that love isn't always a bowl of cherries…

But Mr. Fluckinger and I never talked about any of this. Even when he called me on the phone. I was a bit taken back, of course. A teacher had never phoned me before in my whole life. But he just wanted to invite me to go with him and his family to Paris. He explained that he had told his wife about our conversation after school yesterday and she was the one who suggested that I come to Disneyland with them for a little vacation. I could earn my keep by babysitting his two boys in the evening so they could go out in the city. It sounded great to me and I immediately said yes.

Anyway, I'm back on the couch watching the trash on the news and suddenly Johnny calls. It was kind of ironic because here I was thinking about Mr. Fluckinger thinking about Johnny and within ten minutes I have both of them talking in my ear… my surrogate daddy and the only boy in the universe I wanted to talk to.

Johnny and I must have talked for forty-five minutes. The time flew like a flock of birds going north for summer. Here's what I now know about him from tonight and the five-minute conversation we had on the sidewalk:

He works the night shift in the big post office in Lausanne.
He sorts mail.
He dropped out of law school a year ago.
His father's a lawyer and wanted him to eventually take over the business. He has absolutely no interest in law.
He hates reading law books.
He respects people who sort mail as much as he respects high-powered lawyers.
He wants to read my book, "Don't Bullshit Me Daddy".
He's been on earth four more years than I have.
He has an older brother and a younger sister.
He has no idea what he wants to do when he grows up.
He hopes he never grows up.
He is not sure about climate change, but he is sure that the media have changed.
He reads R. J Ellory's mysteries.
He likes pasta and has been to Italy once with the girl who liked to hit him.
He has never been to America, but he thinks the CIA do lots of bad things.
Last summer he went to the Munich beer festival and got drunk and couldn't remember where his hotel was.
He is not sure if Obama is a good president.
He thinks the world is going to pot.
He doesn't believe in the necessity of having more than three pairs of shoes or underwear.

He likes warm weather.

He likes the "Wing" part of my last name and the idea of flight.

His English is quite good.

He seems to understand when I suddenly jump into English.

About me he knows:

I was born near San Francisco.

I have no family.

My father decided to move to Switzerland shortly after my mother died.

I ask a lot of questions about life.

I have doubts about most things.

I don't trust most ideas about things.

I read a lot of books at a very young age.

I respect snails, butterflies, and monkeys as much as I respect people.

I like living in Switzerland.

I like the perspective living in Switzerland gives me about life in America.

I have no religious upbringing.

I have no idea about the meaning of life.

I have many friends at school, but hardly any "close" friends.

I learned French in about a year, that's no special feat as two-year-olds do it all the time.

I had two birds that are now dead.

I live alone in a large apartment.

I have no idea what I want to do after I finish school.

I have no idea if I want to finish school.
I like school, especially my English teacher.
My English teacher and his wife invited me to go to Disneyland Paris with them.
I walk a lot.
I ski.
I enjoy mountains.
I have a car I have never driven.
I don't know how to drive.
I took a lot of short trips with my father.
I loved my father and mother but really don't remember much about the latter.
My father thought one should have as much freedom as possible about choices concerning one's life and death.
I hate violence.
I don't hate how my father died.

How many times in your life do you talk to somebody when everything seems interesting to both of you? Not very often. Johnny and I seemed to be pretty much interested in the same things, except for the murder mysteries and the CIA.

As we were talking, for whatever reason, I started wondering about how much my mother and father loved each other. I have a hunch quite a bit. Daddy said they were never bored when they were together. Maybe Mommy died before they had a chance to be bored. I don't know. The fact that they decided to have me after they'd been married a long time says something. I think the thing that worked for them was that they were both rather independent, but at the same time they both knew they were dependent on the other. That's what Daddy told me anyway. He said he loved Mommy in such a way that when she was not there he always felt like part of him was missing...

Well, I've known Johnny for exactly fifty minutes. Should I be missing him? I hung up the phone (nobody hangs up a phone anymore...there's no place to hang it...you can't hang a phone in your pocket...) and five minutes later I wanted to be talking to him again. Before we said goodbye, he did slowly but surely invite me to go to a movie on Saturday afternoon. The ball is still rolling. We have a future! Isn't that what life's all about? Having a future... Staying alive... EEE-EEE-EEE... STAYIN' ALIVE! Johnny and I are still alive. At least until Saturday afternoon. I like the idea of a date in the afternoon...And then next week with the Fluckingers in Paris. Disneyland Paris. I'll get to see the Eiffel Tower! And I'll get to see who Mr. Fluckinger has breakfast with every morning, ie his wife!...Daddy once told me that his daddy told him that if ever he was thinking about marrying somebody he should remember that he'll have to look at that woman every morning across the breakfast table. Daddy said his daddy should have also told him to remember that he'll have to talk to the person, too. Daddy told me to remember both things if I ever decided to get married or some such thing.

12

School's out. Another year…Done! Am I a year dumber or a year smarter? I honestly think sometimes school makes people dumber because they start thinking they know things that they really don't know. I celebrated by walking down to Ouchy for a Mövenpick ice cream. Right near the spot where I met Johnny, I bumped into my friend Linda. Actually, she really does bump into people because she' s blind. I first met her two years ago on the sidewalk near my house. She was carrying a bag of groceries and the bag broke. I was behind her and I watched her get down on her hands and knees and grope around for the things that had rolled away. I helped her corral everything and find a new bag. It turned out that her parents lived in the building next to where Daddy and I lived. It also turned out that she gave massages and she gave me one I'll never forget. I guess that's not saying much because it was the only massage I've ever had – at least the only real one where you lie on a table and somebody puts oil on your body and neither the masseur and the massee (my dumb dictionary says this isn't a word, but it obviously should be in a world that made any sense) think that the goal of the whole operation is some kind of eventual sexual stimulation…But the truth was that I did get excited in a way I'll never forget. It was erotic without an object for the eroticism…I just looked

78

up "erotic" in my dictionary…First "eros"…***Eros:*** *Greek Mythology. The god of love, son of Aphrodite.* **Eros:** *n. Psychoanalysis. 1. The sum of all self-preservative, as contrasted with self-destructive, instincts. 2. Sexual drive, libido.* Erotic: *adj. 1. Of or concerning sexual love and desire; amatory* (there's a word I've never met before). *2. Tending to arouse sexual desire. 3. Dominated by sexual love or desire. –n. 1. Rare* **a.** *An amatory* poem (I'll check what amatory means). **b.** *A doctrine of love. 2. An erotic person.* (As expected "amatory" just means "Of, pertaining to, or expressive of love, especially sexual love.")

Love…Love…Love…Will somebody please take me out of my misery and tell me what love is. My guess is that the only way to know what love is is to feel it. You can't describe it. Something tells me I've never really felt it…Not "real" love anyway. Is it possible to put "real" love into words? All the love songs and crap make you want to fall in love, but they don't tell you what it is…Is it possible to love somebody and not try to put it into words? That's probably not possible either…I don't think I loved Cherif. I had a little of the old "eros" sexual desire stuff, but it wasn't the whole package. It was a cheeseburger without the cheese.

Anyway, it was good to see Linda. She's got to be over fifty now and is looking kind of haggard with matted grey hair. She remembered me. She recognized my voice. She told me where she lived which was right close by and said to come over any time. Maybe I will.

The movie was called "Le Cheval du Turin". It was playing in the huge old Lausanne cinema called "Le Capitole". It's the only big movie theater to have survived the modern trend of cutting theaters up into I, II, II, IV, V etc. When the lights came on at the end I realized there were private booths in the back on the ground floor where we were sitting. Movies used to be for more than watching the film. When I pointed them out to Johnny he laughed.

Johnny and I watched the film. There couldn't have been more than ten people in the humongous theater. It was a sunny day and "Le Cheval de Turin" was probably the most boring movie in the history of the cinema. For two and a half hours we watched an old man and his daughter living alone in a small house in the middle of nowhere where the wind blew like crazy constantly. The highlight of their day was the single boiled potato they each had for dinner. The film was in black and white. Johnny had heard it was "thought provoking" and "well done". It actually was both, but that didn't prevent it from being the most boring film I've ever seen. I guess the moral of the story was that life is a bitch. Did Johnny and I need a 150-minute movie to tell us this? I doubt it. The most interesting thing about it all was that, in truth, I was never bored. That was because I kept wondering how Johnny was seeing the film and what was going through his head. Our shoulders bumped a few times. He often changed his position in his chair. Every now and then, he would whisper something to me that was kind of funny and in total opposition to what was going on on the screen. Once he said, "French fries will never taste the same". Another time, "Don't they at least have a kite to go fly."

I won't lie. If you can go to the most boring film in the world with somebody and not be bored, it means something. The question is, did – does – Johnny feel the same way? My guess is that yes, he did, and yes he does. My guess is that Johnny – last name Lang – and I are about to start the greatest love affair in the history of the human heart. My guess is that I will love Johnny and he will love me more than Brad Apricot Pitt and Angelina Blubberlips Jolie ever thought of loving each other, more than Romeo and Juliet ever loved each other, more than Cleopatra and Caesar, more than Tristan and Isolde, more than Mommy and Daddy, more than Mickey Mouse and Minnie Mouse, more than pigs and mud, more than flies and dog shit...

Isn't it fun to believe in God, the Easter Bunny, Santa Claus, and LOVE? Haha! "Haha" might be my favorite word. What in this world isn't "haha"?

So Johnny Lang and I walked out of the dark theater and into the brilliant sunshine of an afternoon in late June. We started ambling downhill – in case you didn't know, Lausanne is a hilly city like San Francisco – and ended up in the garden of the Musée de l'Elysée, the photography museum just behind the Beau Rivage Hotel.

It was obvious neither of us had planned anything for the rest of the day. We sat on a bench at the bottom of the park. We didn't talk much about the movie, but when Johnny said, "At least they had time to get to know themselves", we ended up getting into a long conversation about knowing oneself. Daddy used to trash Socrates' great dictum "Know thyself". He thought it was one of the dumbest things anybody had ever said. He would say, "How can a self know itself? What does it mean to know oneself? One can't know where one's thoughts and desires come from. One can't know the consciousness that is doing the so-called 'knowing' or the unconscious that is making the whole pot boil." His favorite saying was, "Thoughts don't come when I want them to come, but when they want to come". I told Johnny all this and he got kind of animated and said he'd thought about that kind of thing too, but not exactly in the same way.

After a while he invited me for a drink over on the terrace of the Olympic Museum which is next door to the park. To get there you walk on a narrow path that is barely wide enough for a fat person. I walked behind Johnny and liked the back of his head. As we drank our drinks, I said Daddy's other favorite question was "Where did IT all come from?" Johnny laughed. He said he thought the only answer that made any sense was that nothing came from anywhere, that everything always was, that there was no beginning and there will be no end, that there is no need for Genesis, that there is no need for a "Creation", and that everything always has been and will be, and that it all just changes and transforms. I told him Daddy would have agreed with him.

When Johnny said I wasn't like most eighteen-year-olds, I said I wasn't Daddy's daughter for nothing. We started talking about whether or not Daddy was right to fill my head with all these thoughts about life and the mystery of existence and all that crap. Maybe it would have been better if he had taken me to a nice big church that laid out rules in black and white like so many daddies do. Should he have given me a Christian education? A Moslem education? A right-wing education? A left-wing education. Maybe he should he have made me a Buddhist. Maybe he should he have taught me that right and wrong were written on gold tablets like Chuckie's parents drilled into him. Maybe he should have taught me that the American Constitution was divinely inspired and that America was the greatest country on this wild spinning earth.

I told Johnny that it was against Daddy's nature to bullshit me. He just couldn't do it. Did he mess me up? I guess time will tell. Johnny said it was hard as hell to know what makes a good parent.

We ended up having a little dinner on the terrace. Johnny walked me home at about ten. The time went very fast. We all know what that means.

13

I've been thinking a lot about the film Johnny and I saw. Even though it was unbelievably boring, it has stuck like a nail in my head. Maybe most people don't know the origin of the title, "The Horse of Turin". Johnny didn't know it. I only know it because of Daddy. (I've been talking a lot about Daddy lately…I guess I need him.) It comes from a story about the philosopher Nietzsche that Daddy told me about when we were driving through the Black Forest in southern Germany. Supposedly Nietzsche was in Turin in 1889 and saw a man savagely beating his horse with a whip. For whatever reason, this was the last straw for Nietzsche. He couldn't take life anymore. He couldn't stand to see another moment of suffering, cruelty, human stupidity, insanity or whatever. He broke down and didn't talk for the last ten years of his life. Most people said he was crazy. He probably thought it was the other way around. This doesn't mean a whole lot unless you understand what Nietzsche thought about life – at least that's what Daddy said. Many people called him a big bad "pessimist" because he didn't believe in God or life after death and he thought religion and morality were a both big joke. But Daddy said Nietzsche was the total opposite of a pessimist and might actually have been the greatest optimist who has ever lived. I know that may sound stupid, but it's not. Why? O why baby, why?… Because he – Nietzsche – said the real pessimists are the people who say that this world is some kind of secondary world, a world that is just a stepping stone to another higher world. He said Christians were the worst because they live for the next world, for the kingdom of heaven. They see this world as evil, sinful, a test for the next world. Jesus, they say, died to save us from our sins and show us that we would be resurrected. But for Nietzsche, Jesus really said the kingdom of God is the here and now. It wasn't Jesus who talked about resurrection. It was the apostle Paul and his buddies. When Jesus died, the apostles looked at each other and said, "Holy shit, how did that happen? What do we do now?" And then they started all the crap about sin and resurrection and going to hell and a judgment day. But what if there is no resurrection? What if that is all pure fairy tale? What if this world is all there is? Then to live for another world is to waste this life, to sacrifice it to a belief in something that doesn't exist. That, for Nietzsche, was the ultimate sin, the ultimate pessimism.

I know I'm sounding like a hot shit professor or something, but the truth is, this is probably the one thing Daddy told me that has stuck the hardest in my stupid head. I think about it all the time. I think about it every day… And if you don't like it then turn the damn page… Haha!

Anyway, to make a long story drinkable, that's why Mr. Nietzsche saw himself as the ultimate optimist. Because he said "Yes" to this life. This life is all there is.

We must love it. Daddy said Nietzsche was a very sensitive human being. He saw value in every snail, flower, bird, leaf, and horse. He finally couldn't take any more suffering, stupidity, and bullshit. He broke down and spent most of his last ten years in bed staring at the ceiling…

…So Daddy, I listened when you talked. Sometimes anyway. I listened on that trip through the Black Forest. At least I know that the film "The Horse from Turin" was supposed to be inspired by this man Nietzsche. But how? It was two and a half hours of bleakness. Did whoever made the film not understand what Nietzsche really had to say? Nietzsche thought the human race was dumb and weak and greatly lacking in vision. But he knew it was not people's fault. People can't be other than what they are any more than squirrels or trees can be other than what they are. People are part of nature like all the rest. And Nietzsche loved nature because nature is all there is. From what Daddy told me, I don't think Nietzsche would have made a bleak film at all. He would have made a film showing the beauty, mystery, and strange miracle of all life. But he died in 1900. He never made a film or even saw one. He wrote a bunch of books that hardly anybody reads. Daddy read them. Daddy's vision of life was like Nietzsche's. I know. He told me more than once.

I've been thinking about the film because I wonder if it's a typical example of how people are so bad at understanding each other. Daddy used to say Nietzsche was the most misunderstood thinker ever. Should the bleakest film have been the happiest film? Is not believing in anything the first step to believing in everything? What do I believe in? I believe in what I see, what I feel, what I taste and smell. I believe in this life. Another life might be out there…somewhere…but we sure as hell don't know anything about it. I've seen Mommy and Daddy die. Little Laura Winger, has learned to treasure this life. It is all she has, all she knows. If she has to spend her life eating one potato every night, then she will. But if she can eat fruit and vegetables and fondue and spaghetti, then she will. If she can have friends, she will. If she can love somebody, she will. If she can make the earth a beautiful place, she will. But how? How? What can she do with her life? That's the whole reason she's writing this crazy book. How should she spend the time she has left on this earth? She looks at her friends at school. She listens to what they talk about. She looks at how they spend their time, at the music they listen to, at the hours they spend on Facebook and sending messages to each other with their smartphones. But like Nietzsche said…that's life. That's the way people are. That's the world. That's nature. The wonderful world full of lots of beauty and lots of shit…

She wonders a lot about being alone. How alone is she really? How alone is anybody? Most people join the herd…BAAAHHH! When you join the herd, you're not alone. Go to church, go to school, wear the same clothes, listen to the same music, talk the same talk, walk the same walk. Baahhhhh! How alone was her daddy? He definitely wanted to die alone. Did he want to live alone? He had his wife and his daughter. Was that enough? From what he said, his friend Nietzsche was very alone. Was he alone because he couldn't find anyone he could share life with? Is being alone a tragedy? When one shares the world, doesn't it taste better? Aren't two tongues better than one? Aren't four eyes better than two? Aren't two brains better than one? And two hearts…?

Of course little Laura is thinking about little Johnny Lang. Of course she has only known him for a few days. Of course she has the right to dream. Maybe it's not a right, but a necessity…

Good night Laura. Good night Johnny. Good night Mr. Winger. Who says you can't say good night to dead people?

Oh, and don't forget, Laura: tomorrow you're off to Paris. What will that bring? Bring, brang, brung. Bring, brought, brought. Language is so stupid sometimes…It's you and the Fluckingers on the fast train. Take out the "l" and you've got Fuckingers.

Father, forgive me.

Forgive everybody.

We know not what we do.

14

I just spent five days in a tornado. Five days in the biggest most beautiful zoo I've ever seen. Five days in a new book. Five days in a family. Five days in a hot tub of humanity. Five days inside a telescope. I didn't know it was possible to cram so many stimuli into five days. It was like stuffing Beethoven's Fifth, Anna Karenina, the Louvre, and Walt Disney all into the same head at the same time. It was Laura in Wonderland…

I met the Fluckingers on the quai, track 9, on Wednesday morning. We took the early 7h04 TGV. My apartment is literally a two-minute walk from the Lausanne train station. They have two boys aged nine and six, Oscar and Frederic, whom I called "Ozzie" and "Freddie" much to their delight. I haven't spent much time with young boys since I was a kid in California. I had forgotten what species of animal they are. They are funny, crazy, happy, sad; they punch, scream, laugh, tickle; they pretend, pout, imitate, act. And they do it all in a three-minute time span. Three minutes…one round of boxing. These kids never stopped. 14 hours a day – a hundred rounds – Ozzie and Freddie were in the ring. Ozzie, the oldest, seemed like he wanted to please Mommy and Daddy. Freddie, the younger one wanted to get everybody's attention. The battle was on, constantly. Mr. and Mrs. Fluckinger seemed very accustomed to the confusion that reigned whenever the boys were near each other. As soon as we got in the train, they both wanted to sit with me.

I wanna sit next to Laurie…

Her name's Laura.

No, I do…Daddy, you promised.

Promised what?

That I could sit next to her.

We never talked about it.

From Lausanne to Dijon, I had Ozzie and Mr. Fluckinger had Freddie. We switched from Dijon to Paris. Mrs. Fluckinger had a seat by herself in front of her husband.

You take the seat alone dear.

No, you can have it.

Are you sure? Okay.

Mrs. Fluckinger was absolutely everything I had not expected and more. I'd thought she'd be blonde; she had almost black hair except for a few streaks of grey. I'd thought she'd be "petite" with an Audrey Hepburn figure; she was rather tall and had shoulders like a volleyball player. I'd imagined she'd have blue eyes; she had eyes like coffee beans. I'd thought she would be talkative and outgoing; she was very discreet, almost aloof, but not unpleasant to be around. She always seemed to be kind of in her own world, which surprised me too because I had thought Mr. Fluckinger would have a wife with whom he'd be in constant conversation (I guess because in school I always hear him talk). I'm quite sure she had the idea of bringing me along not just to give me – the orphan – a little vacation, but also so she could sit alone in the train and read. Nothing wrong with looking out for yourself a little. She always had a book in her hand. But when the boys got a little out of hand, she would immediately put her book down and shut them up.

Boys, you're in a train. There are other people around.

He told me I looked like a fishstick.

What's wrong with a fishstick? There's nothing wrong with being called a fishstick.

See, I told you.

Talk to Laura and your father.

It was very interesting to see Mr. Fluckinger in a setting that had nothing to do with teaching English. He wore shorts and a T-shirt. He played and joked with the kids. His wife went to the snack bar and brought him back a beer at ten o'clock in the morning. He often had his hand under his shirt to scratch his stomach. When he looked out of the window, he seemed to block out everything around him for a few seconds and dream a quick dream. He was definitely a very kind father and during the four-hour trip, he asked me many times if I wanted or needed anything.

Laura, would you like anything from the snack bar? We forgot to bring things.

No, thanks Mr. Fluckinger. I'm fine. I have a bottle of water.

You brought more than we did.

Not a lot more.

So…magic…Abracadabra…By the time we get to Paris I have a new family! A mommy and daddy and two little brothers! And they have a daughter and a sister! When you've lived alone with your father for nine years, then totally alone for another year, to be suddenly surrounded by four people all the time is like being air-lifted from Death Valley to New York City…

We had to change trains at the Gare de Lyon to get to Disneyland. But we were there and in our hotel by two o'clock. Mr. Fluckinger had reserved a huge room in the Dream Castle Hotel a couple of kilometres from Disneyland. There were bunk beds for the boys and two double beds. I hadn't really thought about it until I saw the room, but I would have thought Mr. and Mrs. Fluckinger might have wanted a little privacy, given they had a babysitter along. But no, we were all together…

Mommy, I want the top bed.

No, I do.

I'm older.

That's why you should sleep on the bottom.

Whadayamean, that's why I should sleep on the top.

Maybe Laura wants it.

You don't want it, do you Laurie?

Her name's Laura.

She said I could call her Laurie.

Did she? If you keep fighting I'll take the top bunk and Daddy will sleep underneath.

By three o'clock we were walking down Main Street in the park. Everything was like in America, except there were fewer fat people and people were speaking French. You've got to hand it to Mr. Walter Disney. His whole idea was to make life fun. Fun! Fun! Fun! Happy! Happy! Happy! Nobody fretting, worrying, and gnashing any teeth over the meaning of life or politics or religion! Life has one goal: GOOD CLEAN FUN! Mr. Disney wanted you to think about two things only: what ATTRACTION you're going to do next and where you are going to get the next thing to put in your mouth! He had it all figured out. Amuse the masses and keep their stomachs full. Nobody's thinking about Nietzsche or their dead dog or the wars in Syria and Afghanistan. Nobody's thinking about the people starving in Africa. Nobody's worrying about whether or not Johnny Lang loves Laura Winger. All anybody's thinking is about fun and food. F & F. You don't have time to get bored. Nobody stays for more than a couple of days. Maybe that's the way life should be. Quick in. Quick out. I'll bet Disney was never bored when he created it all. I'll bet he didn't spend five minutes ruminating about suffering, injustice, the existence of God, the meaning of life, etcetera...etcetera. I'll bet he just lived! And I'll bet he was thankful for every second he was alive! I'll bet that if on the same damn day his mommy died, his daddy died, his canaries died, two hundred and ninety-nine people died in a plane crash, ten thousand people starved to death, nine million cows were slaughtered to make hamburgers, and ten thousand Italians died in an earthquake, Walt Disney would still be trying to think up new ways to make people... HAPPY!!!

No matter how much shit was going on, I'll bet he'd still say, "YOU HAVE TO LIVE, LAURA! YOU HAVE TO GET UP IN THE MORNING, LAURA! GOD OR NO GOD, MEANING OR NO MEANING, TRUTH OR NO TRUTH, BORING SCHOOL OR NO BORING SCHOOL, YOU, LAURA WINGER HAVE TO DO SOMETHING WITH YOUR LIFE! AND YOU MIGHT AS WELL MAKE IT AS GOOD AND HAPPY AS POSSIBLE! MAKE THE WORLD YOUR DISNEYLAND, LAURA. MAKE IT YOUR LAURALAND!!!

That's what I thought about that first day in Disneyland. But I must admit I was having fun while I was doing it. Ozzie and Freddie were in heaven. It's possible Mr. Fluckinger was having more fun than anybody else. He reminded me of Daddy when he took me to Disneyland after Mommy died. He ran from ride to ride with his boys. He acted scared on the fast rides. He licked his ice cream cone. He kept saying, "Come on boys...come on Laura...let's do The Pirates of the Caribbean!"...or whatever ride caught his eye.

Mrs. Fluckinger seemed to have a different idea of fun. She spent most of her time sitting on a bench observing people or reading. We'd leave her some place and report back in an hour or so. The boys didn't seem to mind. They had their daddy and me to run around with.

That night for dinner we sat in a place called New Orleans Square and ate hamburgers and French fries while we listened to a Dixieland band. We got back to the hotel at about ten. The boys were dead tired. I was the last one to use the bathroom. I had checked my messages on my telephone. Johnny was there, twice. Mr. Fluckinger was asleep when I came out of the bathroom. His wife was reading in bed.

Before I fell asleep I thought about the place of Disneyland in the "real" world. But then I thought what an idiot I was. Disneyland is as much a part of the "real" world as anything else. It's as real as a machine gun or a chicken with its head cut off. It's as real as a gunshot in the ghetto or a kiss on a sidewalk in the rain. It's all real. Even fantasy is real. Somebody has to think it up. Did I like Disneyland? I loved it. Did Ozzie and Freddie like Disneyland? They can't wait to go back. Did Mr. and Mrs. Fluckinger like Disneyland? I'm sure he loved his boys in Disneyland. I had no idea how she felt.

Good night everybody. Somewhat of a change from saying good night to nobody.

The next morning at breakfast Mr. and Mrs. Fluckinger decided we'd all take the train back in to Paris. It's only a half-hour ride. The boys bitched for a few minutes, but Mommy promised them the first thing we'd do was go up to the top of the Eiffel Tower. Daddy promised them we'd be back in Disneyland in the afternoon. I think more than anything they wanted me to see Paris, to feel Paris, to smell Paris, to breathe Paris. They'd been there dozens of times.

We did a whirlwind tour. We took the metro from the Gare de Lyon to the Eiffel Tower. We walked through the Tuillerie Gardens. We went in the Louvre for an hour. We ambled along the Seine and had lunch in a restaurant near Notre Dame. We were back at the hotel at four. Mrs. Fluckinger decided to stay in the hotel and rest. We would all meet for dinner in the hotel at nine.

What did you think of Paris, Laura?

It's the most beautiful city I've ever seen.

Really? Not too many tourists?

I don't mind tourists? I'm a tourist.

You don't seem to mind much, Laura.

You don't either, Mr. Fluckinger.

Hey boys, what do you want to do first?

The Jungle Boat ride!

No, I want to do that train again!

Let's do the Jungle Boat. We haven't done that yet.

Oscar always gets his way!

No he doesn't. Nobody always gets their way.

You do Daddy.

That's what you think.

So your wife wasn't feeling too well.

No, she was just tired.

After the Jungle Boat ride we went to Frontierland to a place called Tom Sawyer Island. The boys played while Mr. Fluckinger and I sat on a bench and made sure they didn't kill themselves or each other. Sometimes when you sit on a bench with someone nothing happens. Other times the bench might become an electric chair, a love seat, a psychiatrist's couch, or a confession booth. This bench became a microscope.

Thanks for coming, Laura.

I'm really enjoying it. It's rather strange to actually be in a "family".

It's strange for me sometimes, too.

How do you mean?

Once you're in it, it's very hard to get out.

Unless it's just you and your father and he dies.

He kept looking straight ahead, but he smiled a half-smile.

I'm a father who is still alive.

Fortunately.

For whom?

For your wife and kids. For your students.

For the kids yes. For my students?...Oh, that's an interesting question. As, for my wife...

For whatever reason my ears perked up like a German Shepherd's when it hears a noise outside a door.

Of course for your wife.

Ten seconds slowly ticked by. He turned his head in my direction, but it didn't quite get to my face.

That's what I like about the year 2012. Very few things are shocking anymore. Especially for eighteen-year-olds. It's probably easier to tell you things than people my age or older.

What are you talking about? What do you mean?

I looked at him, my teacher. It was hot. He lifted his T-shirt and did the stomach scratching thing. He put his other hand to his mouth and kind of cough-chuckled.

I might as well tell you, Laura. I see no reason not to. My wife doesn't love me anymore, and – if you want to know the truth - I don't love her. There's no sense in loving somebody who has stopped loving you. She loves women. A woman. She didn't tell me until after Frederic was born, but I could feel it coming. I knew it was going to rain. The clouds had been forming for years and had been getting thicker and thicker.

My immediate thought was about how this guy always seemed so "happy" in the classroom in front of us students. He was always in a good mood. He always had a smile on his face. He gave his heart and soul to us. And here he was living with a woman who was as foreign to him as a Chinese passport. I didn't say anything.

Of course it's not the end of the world. Nobody's dead. In our family I mean. But the question so many people have to deal with is, what do you do when you have children and love is gone, and – in this case – when your wife's a lesbian? Do you sacrifice for the kids? Do you stay together and try to figure out ways to keep yourself from losing your mind? Do you toss love in the garbage and find a substitute or substitutes? Probably three-fourths of the couples of the world with kids have to find answers to these questions.

I realized this was probably the first time I had seen Mr. Fluckinger really serious. In school he'd always say things in such a way that kept us amused. This wasn't amusing. It was something else. I finally opened my mouth.

I'm glad you feel like you can talk to me, Mr. Fluckinger.

I hadn't planned to.

Do many other people know this?

Not many. A couple of friends.

You always seem so happy in class.

I want my students to feel good. You learn more when you feel good.

Not necessarily.

Maybe not about life, but about school crap.

The boys were climbing, jumping, swinging, and shouting and not bothering a soul. Disney does it again. We were speaking English. I don't think I had ever heard him use the word "crap" before.

I guess so.

It is interesting that I can talk to you, Laura. But really, why shouldn't I be able to talk to you? School is out. We've seen each other almost every day for two years. You're eighteen. You're an adult. You've been through more than most forty-year-olds have.

Well, maybe not...

Yes you have. And for two years you've shown me what kind of person you are.

I have?

Sure you have.

What kind of a person do you think I am?

He paused a few seconds before he spoke.

Before your parents died, they obviously gave you a certain way of looking at things.

My mother didn't really have time to. But I'm sure

watching her die made me watch myself live...if you see what I mean.

Of course.

And I wouldn't say my father "gave me" a certain ways of looking at things. I'd say more like he "left the door open" to a lot of possibilities. He never told me "what" to think. He tried to tell me "how" to think.

I had never realized this until I said it. A lot of things are like that.

That's what I mean. He gave you a very open mind.

Sometimes I'm not so sure it's such a good thing. I'm really not. Sometimes I look at people who are all dogmatic and everything and have principles tattooed all over their bodies, and I think, "Gee, wouldn't it be nice to believe in God and truth and the Ten Commandments and all that.

Which God would you like to believe in?

That's the problem.

Laura, I think if anybody can handle so much freedom at a young age, it's you. The fact that I just told you that the mother of those two boys out there (he aimed a forefinger) was in love with a woman means a lot. I didn't plan to tell you, but I realize now that I did tell you because I thought you were somebody who could actually "hear" me. There aren't many somebodies like that.

I suddenly thought about the time when we had talked alone together in class after school, when I had wondered if maybe I was the object of some intricate plan of seduction – the cute fatherless motherless female student, seemingly easy prey for the cool teacher. And now the cool teacher has a gay wife. But he didn't have a plan. Not then. Not now. He had found somebody to talk to.

Well, thanks.

You're situation is really quite amazing, Laura. Your parents dying, your father leaving the world an open book, nobody looking over your shoulder. Most kids' stories are kind of already written for them.

Maybe mine's just written in a different way.

Well, you weren't raised a Moslem in Marrakesh or a Mormon in Salt Lake City or a Hindu in Calcutta…

Some Moslems blow up buildings and others are very nice people. Some Mormons are closed-minded jerks and others are pretty good guys. What I mean is that one's education doesn't guarantee anything. Two people might be given the same set of rules, but use them in totally different ways. Every kid plays with his toys differently. Just look and Oscar and Freddie out there.

You're right, of course. There's just something about your situation that is unique.

For whatever dumb reason, I thought of his wife back in the hotel room stretched out on the bed. Were her clothes on or off? Was she curled up or spreadeagled on her back? How did Mr. Fluckinger "see" his wife? And then – do you know what? – the boys came running over. They had had enough of Tom Sawyer Island. They wanted to do something else.

15

I just realized Europeans have no idea what Americans are like and vice versa. I've been reading newspapers and talking to people at school and they all think Mitt Romney is some whacked out religious freak who doesn't give a shit about anything but Mormons and money. They think Obama is the closest thing to Jesus since Martin Luther King. What I see is that they see American politics in black and white. Obama good, Romney bad. I still haven't heard a European say one nice word about Romney or one bad word about Obama. What they never think about is that neither Romney or Obama are bad guys...they're both just caught up in the big dirty washing-machine of American politics. It sounds to me like they both just talk a lot of crap to keep their customers satisfied. Obama never closed Guantanamo and hasn't stopped the war in Afghanistan. Romney likes his cash (what American doesn't?) and thinks giving a person a job is better than giving a person money. Nothing really wrong with that. But of course I'm simplifying things. Isn't that what the politicians do? Isn't that what everybody does with everything. I'm starting to believe that the dumber a person is, the more she simplifies things. The smarter you are, the more you see how everything is very complicated. Does that mean dumb people rule the world? Maybe. Or maybe they're smart people who realize that the dumb masses want simple answers so they talk to them like they're idiots so they'll stay idiots and vote for them. Before Daddy died, every now and then we'd talk about all this junk.

I wonder if people will ever understand each other. Maybe "understanding" someone is not only impossible, but also a stupid thing to want to do. It's like if you take an apple and dissect everything and analyze it under a microscope, there will be nothing left to eat. Will Mr. Fluckinger ever understand why his wife became a lesbian? Will I ever understand why Mr. Fluckinger was a perfect gentleman on that bench in Disneyland and made no effort whatsoever to seduce me? Will I understand why Johnny Lang sends me all these nice messages and when I read them I feel warm and happy like Christmas is coming? When you really get down and think about it, we never really know "why" anything happens or "who" anybody is, including our delicious selves. But most people act like they pretty much know "why" everything happens and "who" everybody is because they've simplified everything like the politicians do. Me, I'm for both Obama and Romney; I love Obama's ears and I think Romney has the best haircut in America. And they have two of the cutest smiles on the face of the earth...

The trip to Paris showed me I'm as dumb as everybody else. Here I had thought Mr. Fluckinger was the happiest man in the world and now I realize he's one of the saddest. I had thought being an only child and an orphan at eighteen was a pretty lousy thing to happen to somebody, but then I wondered what will happen to Freddie and Ozzie when they learn about the "truth" of their mommy and daddy. I started thinking maybe it wasn't so bad being Laura Winger.

It's Sunday. All day. We got back three days ago. What have I done since then? Listen to music, walk, eat, think, read, go to the swimming pool, wait for Johnny to send me a message, and feed Natasha's cat. She and her family are in Greece for a week and I volunteered to feed Dvoràk. Have you ever heard a better name for a cat? And what a cat! Dvoràk got hit by a car a few months ago. His whole rear end was messed up and his tail didn't work anymore. It just hung down like a dead snake. He had about five operations – including one to cut off his tail – and now he's back in business being a crazy tiger cat again. According to Natasha he is a serial killer and averages a mouse a day. I can confirm this. In the two days I have been feeding him, he has left three mice for me on the doorstep. Why doesn't he eat them so I don't have to give him his smelly cat food? I don't know. This morning I wrote a poem about him:

No one knows what happens in the heart.
The heart, like all existence, is a great mystery.
I do not own my heart; if anything, my heart owns me.
My heart will stop beating when it wants to, not when I

want it to, unless I shoot myself in the head like Daddy did or get hit by a train or some such rigamorole.

One night in bed I realized that my heart was not attached to anything like a power generator or a battery. It just beats. And beats. And beats. It has no outside help. From that night on I understood that my heart is as special as the universe. It just is.

I'm not sure if the heart has anything to do with love, except that no one knows what happens in love either.

Most hearts beat much longer than most loves, and much more steadily.

Without a heart you die. Can the same be said for love?

I recently asked my biology teacher if worms have hearts. They do, she said, but their hearts are shaped differently and their blood is not like our blood.

So what? I thought. A heart is a heart. Blood is blood.

Dvoràk, a friend's cat that I am feeding, has killed three mice in two days.

They have hearts, those mice, and crimson blood.

Dvoràk is a serial killer with a heart.

No one knows what happens in the heart.

Lately I've been listening to a lot of Daddy's CDs. Maybe it's some kind of unconscious homage marking the anniversary of his death. He liked mostly classical stuff. But he also liked Bob Dylan and the Beatles. This morning while I was eating breakfast I put on Rachmaninov's third piano concerto. It is the most insane piece of music I have ever heard in my life. I don't mean insane like it made me go crazy, but the fact that it goes on and on and the piano player plays like he has twenty fingers. I just googled it to see how many notes the soloist had to memorize – as far as I know they never have sheet music in front of them. 29,035 notes! Can you imagine that? 29,035 notes perfectly memorized in one human head! And he probably has all Beethoven's concertos in there, too, and all Chopin's stuff, and on and on. It was the idea of the human head that made me crazy. I wonder if people with brains that can do this kind of thing get along better or worse with "the rest of life". Do they have an easier time with love and going to the grocery store and dealing with friends and family? Or are they royal pains is the asses because they see everything as infinitely complicated and they think they're smarter than everybody else and have no real friends and are lonely as hell?

After Rachmaninov, I put on some Bob Dylan called "Pure Dylan". He sounded like he's a really nice guy, but a really lonely guy too. He probably wanted to save the world when he was young, then when he realized he couldn't do it, he started being obsessed with love. If you can't help everybody, at least you can love somebody! But from his music, I don't think most of his loves lasted very long. One song, "If You See Her Say Hello", almost had me in tears. Actually it had me "in a tear". My left eye got watery.

On our last day in Disneyland there was a moment when I watched Mr. Fluckinger look at his wife and kids across the dinner table. He and I were on one side and

Mrs. Fluckinger was on the other side sitting between the boys. Ozzie was talking about how "Pirates of the Caribbean" had been his favorite ride. Then Freddie started in about what he liked best. It must have gone on for two or three minutes. Our food hadn't come yet. We were just sipping our drinks. Mr. Fluckinger's eyes went from one boy to the other and then finally froze somewhere in the middle of his wife's chest. His mouth was closed and his teeth seemed glued. I got the feeling he was seeing all the illusions of the world get blown to smithereens. You believe in things; they prove phoney or false. You start with Santa Claus. It's not so bad when you find out he's a fake because you've still got all the goodies your parents have given you. Then you fall in love with some kid in school. When that blows up it's a little more serious. But the sea is full of fish, so you survive. Then you get older and your best friend turns out not to be a best friend. Maybe she stole your boyfriend or said a few things behind your back. But you find another best friend. Then, like Bob Dylan, you want to save the world, but you realize you can't. You wonder why God isn't saving it. Then God follows Santa Claus out the window. Then you have a beautiful marriage with champagne and a honeymoon and you make a couple of cute kids. But then your wife turns out to be a lesbian. A few years later one of your kids becomes a drug addict and the other starts getting bad grades in school. Then your grandpa falls off a horse and breaks his neck. He dies. Grandma can't live without him, so she dies. Then another ugly war breaks out in the Middle East. Then your mommy's blood gets out of whack and she drops in a grave. Then Daddy...Stop the world! Let me get off!...I'm on your side Mr. Fluckinger. I'm with you all the way. Shit happens. I don't really want to get off the merry-go-round. It's all we have. It's all we have. It's all we...

16

It's time. Finally. It's time for me to write down Daddy's death. For a year I couldn't do it. I couldn't even think about doing it. I was all emotion. One big pile of sadness that still had to go to school and say hello to people and take tests and eat lunch and pretend I cared about whether Johnny Depp and Vanessa Paradis still loved each other. I couldn't write about how Daddy died, where Daddy died, what Daddy said before he died. I had to write about all the other stuff, like school and Mr. Fluckinger and Johnny. I could write a little about Daddy's life. But not his death...not D-E-A-T-H. Not how he said goodbye to life. Not about his last words to me before he wandered into a forest and turned his brain into a mini firework. Pop. Fly. Sizzle. Float to the ground. Disappear. Forever.

I've held it in long enough. The emotional bubble has to break. Words, human words have to come out. The first anniversary of William Winger's death has to be marked on the great calendar of time, stupid time that constantly slips out of your hands like a greasy fish.

But when I talk now about his death, I'm really talking about his life. What does death mean without life? Nothing. Death is just the stupid exclamation point at the end of the story. The exclamation point means nothing without the story.

And let's face it…I'm also talking about me, his one and only survivor. Me, not-so-little-anymore Laura Jezabel Winger, the only baby he made out of all those times he made love. The only sperm that hit the house and squeezed in through the door and created a "family". I'm the only one who knows the story. If I don't tell it nobody will:

The Death of William Winger
by Laura Winger

You only have one daddy. You might pretend you have two if your mommy remarries or something, but there's only one man and one woman who made each of us. They live for a while and then they die.

My daddy's name was William and nobody called him Bill. I don't know why. Nobody called him Will or Willie either. Everybody except me called him William. I called him Daddy.

When he was sixty-five or sixty-six (I'm not sure which it was and it doesn't matter at all) he got very sick inside the music box. There are lots of instruments in there and if one of them starts playing false notes it can be contagious and pretty soon not only are the violins messing up, but the bassoons, flutes, oboes, drums, cellos, and basses are all playing wrong notes too. Even the harp can start sounding like somebody is scratching a blackboard. All the music becomes just a crazy cacophony. Sometimes the conductor gives up, walks off the stage, and the symphony is over.

If you're one who likes calendars, Daddy died on the seventeenth of July in the year two thousand and eleven. I'm not a fan of calendars because all they do is make time look finite and understandable, kind of like alphabets and words do with the rest of existence. The number two thousand and eleven doesn't mean jack shit because there was no beginning of time. Jesus wasn't the beginning of time. Neither were the Jews, or the Gentiles, or the American Constitution. By the way, Daddy was born across the ocean in California.

So things were going so wrong in Daddy's organ orchestra that he finally went to the big hotel full of sick people up at the top of Lausanne. They put him in a room in a metal bed with lily white sheets, crisp like crackers. There were other sufferers in the room too. Daddy talked a little to people around him and over him and they gave him some tests and medicine and put needles in his skin. He stayed for a few nights. The hotel bill was terrible. I know because I got it after Daddy died. One day a man in a suit came and told Daddy that they were going to open the music box and take out an instrument and try to tune up a violin or two and that there was a chance that the music might start sounding a little better, but there was no guarantee. Daddy left the hospital and came home. He told me that the last place in the world he wanted to be, the last place he wanted to see, was the inside of that building up at the top of Lausanne.

He wanted to die where there was beauty all around, not in a hospital.

Daddy and I lived together in our apartment on the Boulevard de Grancy for another two weeks. His face got thinner and it got harder for him to walk downstairs to go to the COOP to buy some bread or cheese or vegetables. He listened to a lot of music during those fourteen days. We talked less and he ate less. The music got softer. One day he listened to Tchaikovsky's Sixth symphony and then he turned off the stereo. I went to the swimming pool with Natasha for a couple of hours. When I came back there was a note saying he had taken a taxi to the forest above Pully where we could find him so we wouldn't waste time looking where he wasn't. He said he'd be near the bridge and the stream.

I don't know who gave him the gun. What were his options? Standing in front of a train. Poison. A rope around the neck. He didn't want to suffer anymore. It just came down to that. That, and the fact that he always said he never wanted to be a burden to me. Or to anybody else for that matter.

The last thing Daddy said before I left to go to the swimming pool was, "It looks like a very nice day. Enjoy it, Laura."

I realize now why I had him cremated. You don't want to put somebody in a coffin whose head has been blown to pieces.

17

Do romantic places help make romantic things happen? Does romance happen when it wants to happen regardless of where you are? Maybe if you try to create a romantic setting, odds are it will fall flat. Are romantic moments as unpredictable as dice on a craps table?

Last night Johnny took me to dinner in a restaurant in Chexbres called "Le Tavernier". It is far and away the most "romantic" place I've ever seen in my life. There is this absolutely breathtaking outdoor terrace that overlooks the vineyards and Lac Leman and the Alps are posing naked on the other side of the lake just waiting to get their picture taken. Not only that, there's a waterfall that runs off the terrace. I'm sure he had to reserve a table because it was a perfect night and you didn't need a sweater even after all the stars came out. Switzerland gives you about ten nights a year like this.

Most of the couples around us looked like they were either madly in love or desperately trying to fall in love – that is, one person was trying to persuade the other person that together they would be the happiest couple on earth. I ask, "What is love?" But everybody knows that love is what gets tattooed on your brain or bicep or both the first time it happens. Everybody knows that love is the hole in your tummy while you're waiting for the phone to ring. Everybody knows that love is that kiss that feels like the four lips have been in the oven all day. Everybody knows that it's looking in the mirror just one more stupid time before you walk out the door to meet your Romeo or Juliet. Or when every day feels like Christmas. Or when just the thought of the person makes certain body parts melt…That's love…until it all turns to…SHIT! I've seen it happen a million times. I might be stupid, but at least I know that the chances of love lasting are about as good as a duck flying to the moon. We all might be stupid, but in today's world, everybody over eighteen knows that love…rarely…endures…forever.

So what happened when Johnny and I were sitting on the moonlit terrace of Le Tavernier last night staring at each other like duck hunters looking down the barrels of their shotguns? Did we jump into Lake Love with all our clothes on? Were we already in love and this was just the seal of confirmation? What did I want? What did he want? Did we want the same things? Do people in love always think they want the same things? Maybe the secret to love is wanting different things? Cherif and I wanted different things and that pumpkin exploded. I don't know what love is any more than a duck knows how far it is to the moon. I know what love isn't. I know when I don't love somebody. That has happened. Three times. Marcel Monney, Cherif, and Chuckie. But how do you know when you do love somebody? Johnny put his hand across the table. I took it…

I love you Laura.

Don't bullshit me Johnny.

I'm not bullshitting you Laura.

How do you know you love me?

You don't know it. You feel it.

What do you feel?

That every time I'm with you I'm happy and I want to see you again as soon as we separate.

Are you sure that's love? Maybe it just means you're lonely.

Everybody's lonely.

That's probably true. So we're all just trying to fill up a big hole. Maybe you're just trying to fill up your hole Johnny.

Maybe I am. But that doesn't mean I don't love you.

Who do you think needs a bigger shovel, you or me?

I don't know.

Have you noticed the people around us? Most of them look like they're in heat. Is being in heat being in love?

I don't know. Maybe.

How many of these people will want to be with – will be with – the person on the other side of the table in three years' time? In five years? In five months? In five days?

I don't know. It doesn't matter.

How many do you think have said "I love you" tonight?

I don't know.

But you say you know you love me…

I don't know what got into me. I wasn't trying to be mean. I was just trying to be me. I'll tell you what happened in a minute.

18

The American ambassador to Libya got killed. So did three other Americans working with him. Some people are saying some Muslims were mad about a film that made fun of their prophet. They stormed the embassy with guns and grenades. The ambassador had tried to help the country get on the right track. What is the right track? Killing four people for a film they had nothing to do with surely can't be the right track. Romney's a Mormon. People make fun of his prophet all the time. And his underwear. And his polygamous ancestors. Mormons don't kill because of it. The real reason for the killing couldn't have been a lousy film. It had to be elsewhere, deep deep down in the depths of the killers' lives. Deep deep down, like where I look when I wonder why I talked to Johnny the way I did that night at Le Tavernier. He tells me he loves me and I tell him to cut the bullshit… After Cherif, am I afraid that I'll always fall "out of love" and so I'm afraid to fall "in love"? Johnny's a good guy. He's cute. He's not too hung up on himself. Most of the time I enjoy talking to him. After Le Tavernier we kissed for a while in his car. We kissed when he brought me home. But something was missing. That's the thing…something is missing. How often is nothing missing? How often are things perfect? How often is there a total fusion with the other person or with

116

whatever you're doing. After Daddy died I listened to Tchaikovsky's 6th Symphony, the one he listened to the day he shot himself in the head. I'll bet he fused with that Fourth Movement, that last note from the cello string that fades away into nothing. You can fuse with life; you can fuse with death. Can I fuse with Johnny? I don't think so. And it's not that I haven't tried. We made love that night after Le Tavernier. He came up to the apartment. I shouldn't say "we" made love. Maybe "he" made love. But it takes two to really make love. I was not all there. Part of me didn't let him in. I like Johnny. I really do. I've liked him since the first time I saw him on the sidewalk going down to Ouchy. I waited for his phone call. We exchanged words, messages. We held hands, we kissed, we had what the human world calls "sex". But we didn't make "love". It's nothing he has said or done. It's just the way the bodies mix. I could probably live with Johnny. I could probably have children with Johnny. I could probably be reasonably happy with Johnny. But if I told him I loved him, I'd be bullshitting him. I'm eighteen. Almost nineteen. I've learned two things in this life: we all die and we rarely truly love.

19

So what happened? I gave it another try. The last try? Maybe. Probably. The same something was missing. I told Natasha about it. She listened, but she has her own problems. My situation isn't a problem; it's a fact. You can't force yourself to fuse with another person. You can't force yourself to fuse with music, with school, with books, with life, with death, with the damn sandwich you eat for lunch. Either it happens or it doesn't.

Laura, I love you.

Johnny, there's something missing.

For me there isn't.

I know. You've told me. But there's no other way I can put it.

Things can take time.

Maybe time can take things.

What do you mean?

I don't know. I just said it.

20

Sometimes I think I talk to Daddy more when he's dead than when he was alive. Every time I read a newspaper or watch the news on TV, I talk to him about it. The world is insane. Another American soldier in Afghanistan got killed by an Afghan soldier he was supposed to be helping train. There have been dozens of such killings. I have an Afghan friend in school. Her parents fled in the 1990s. She says the people there don't care a bit about democracy. They just want to eat and be left in peace. Syria gets worse all the time. How can that tall skinny president keep killing his own people? Kofi Annan tried to help. Nothing. Now there's another mediator in there. Nothing. He said the tall skinny president is committing crimes against humanity. Who else could he be committing crimes against – Martians? Large poultry? Termites??? Some of the Muslims are still mad about the stupid film. They're taking to the streets. China is mad at Japan for taking over some island nobody lives on. Obama and Romney are throwing punches below the belt. Here in Lausanne people get beat up in the streets at night for no reason. A friend of Marcel Monney's was walking home at eleven-thirty the other night and got punched and kicked by a band of thugs. In Switzerland? In Switzerland. A dirty banker gets out of jail and the American government gives him $104,000,000 for ratting on other dirty people. William and Kate are mad because pictures were taken of Kate's bare chest. Why is her chest different from her face? She loves to have pictures taken of her face…

I'm mad. It's one of those days. When you're mad, things that would normally just bounce off your head end up crawling around in your brain and playing havoc.

Why am I mad? Because I can't be with the one I love. I saw him yesterday in the grocery store. When I saw him I knew I loved him. He was with his sons. His wife wasn't there. We talked for a couple of minutes in the aisle between the canned tomatoes and the pickles. I think he loves me, too. We've known each other for two years. Why did it take so long? Because we're not supposed to love each other. He's married. He's older. He's my teacher. Society doesn't like that kind of thing. But I'm starting to not like society. I'm starting to think I should ignore society. Is that possible? Where in the universe is it written that one has to be part of the society one happens to be born into? Of course you have to be polite to people on the bus and pay your bills and your taxes and not steal stuff. But if you do all that, can't you say, "Screw all the bullshit…I'll live in my own world"? If I don't want to think about Afghanistan and Syria and the tall skinny president, who says I have to think about them? If I don't want to read about Kate's chest or even have an opinion about it, can't I do that? I don't have to listen to the Republicans and Democrats tell lies about each other. I can change the channel whenever I want to.

Sure you have to live in the world. But what world? Do any two people see the world the same way? I doubt it. For every human head, there is a world. I'll take mine and go where I want to with it. I'll run away. I'll hide in a cave. I'll climb a mountain. I'll see what I want to see and let other people see what they want to see. If I want to look at flowers instead of slaughterhouses, that's my choice. If I want to listen to Dvoràk (not the cat) instead of watching CNN, that's my choice. I can't change the bullshit, but I don't have to live in it either…

Run, Laura, run…

Where…alone?

21

Summer has almost melted away. School starts in two weeks. Natasha went to Greece with her parents. She came home with a major headache. She thinks she might be pregnant. She wouldn't be the first female to go to Santorini on vacation and come home with an extra passenger inside herself. She said she doesn't really remember what happened. Too much ouzo in a discotheque called The Black Beach. A man. A walk in the moonlight that ended on the sand. She said her period's five days late. I told her mine has been late a couple of times, but it eventually always shows up. I asked her if she got the guy's name and phone number just in case. She said he had hers but not vice versa. It often happens that way. Johnny had mine, but I didn't have his. Speaking of whom, he hasn't called for two weeks. No messages. No emails. Is he trying to punish me for saying I didn't love him? But we were running out of things to talk about. I wonder if that happens to monkeys and elephants.

I hope Natasha's not pregnant. Her parents would either disown her or put her in a convent. That's what she said anyway. What do monkey and elephant parents do when one of their daughters gets pregnant a little early in life? I'll bet they love them even more and celebrate with a few bananas. People are hard on each other. People might be the wildest animals on earth. All the junk on the internet makes me think so. There are some beautiful things, but there's a lot more garbage than gold. The election is starting to make me sick. I'm not supposed to let things make me sick. Obama and Romney have got bloody noses. Both are trying so desperately to say the right things to pull the undecided voters to their side. I heard an American interviewed on the Swiss radio the other day say that he won't vote in a presidential election until a candidate says that "God DOESN'T bless America - or if He does, He doesn't bless it more any other country in the world." That was the first intelligent thing I'd heard on the subject in a month. The commentator said it'll be a long wait before he votes…

What time is it? It's past my bedtime…and Daddy's deadtime…I can hear myself think. My brain's talking too much. Somebody turn off the sound…

22

I know part of the reason why I don't love Johnny. He finally called. He started giving me this long speech about how he was sure that 9/11 was an inside job done by the CIA and Bush. It's all over the internet, he said. You're full of shit, I said. He was insistent. He knew. He had read. The Towers couldn't have come down on their own. There's proof the American government did it. Yeah, I said, just like there's proof that God exists. He went on and on. Was he trying to seduce me with idiocy? I stopped listening and started thinking about something Daddy and I used to talk about: now that a lot of people have stopped believing that God or the Devil are the cause for everything, they have to come up with some other cause to satisfy their unquenchable thirst to know. So now we get all these absurd conspiracy theories that infest the internet. Daddy used to say the same thing happened with the ancient Greeks. First they had all their gods running around that "caused" everything — gods of love, war, sea, weather, fertility…you name it, the gods were making it happen! Then Plato and his buddies came along and they stopped believing in this nonsense, but had to replace it with their own version of "the truth". They couldn't admit that they didn't know the truth; they had to come up with new truth. More bullshit. More refined bullshit. But still bullshit…Anyway, when I heard all this crap coming out of Johnny's mouth, I knew I didn't love him and that I never would love him. So much in this world comes down to who - whom? (who gives a shit?...I'll ask my English teacher...) – you can talk to. And to talk to somebody you have to have some kind of shared vision of what this life is – or isn't – all about. Daddy said that's why that guy Nietzsche died with no friends and why people on the People Pages have lots of people at their funerals.

After Johnny told me about the 9/11 conspiracy, he asked me who (whom?) I was going to vote for. I told him I agreed with the guy on the radio and that I wasn't going to vote for anybody until one of them said God wasn't blessing America. When I told him I was thinking about checking out of the world and living in my own world, a world where there were no gods taking sides in arguments and no bullshit "truths" polluting everything, he said, "But Laura, you say you know the truth about 9/11." I said, "No Johnny, I didn't say that. I just said I thought your truth was bullshit..."

There's so much of it...so much bullshit... The other day I heard an interview on the radio with a guy who was studying human sleep patterns. He kept saying "We don't know why this is"..."We don't know why that is..." "We don't know why people sleep at all and, why old people need less sleep." I suddenly thought this is the whole problem with the world...everybody wants to know WHY...Why did the price of gas go up? Why did he do that? Why did she say that? Why do we sleep? Why do rabbits shit all over the place? Why don't I love Johnny? Why did Daddy die? Because he shot himself in the head…But why did he shoot himself in the head? Because he was in pain…But why was he in pain? Because he had cancer…But why did he get cancer? Because…because…because…And why is there something and not nothing? Why do I ask these questions and get one answer and the terrorist killers who did the 9/11 attacks get another answer? Why don't I love Johnny? Because we don't share the same view of life. Why don't we share the same view of life? Why do I ask all these questions and other people don't? Why do Republicans believe this and Democrats believe that? Why is the earth still spinning? Because that's what it does…but why? Why? Why?…And you know what? Maybe there is no answer to any WHY question. Maybe that is the only thing that is really TRUE. All answers are cheap answers, half answers, answers to satisfy all us idiots…People Page answers…nickel and dime answers….

I'll shut up. Anyway, tomorrow I'll blow up all this bullshit because I'm going to tell you who I love and why. Haha, ha…ha.

23

But you already know who I love. You knew it when I said I've known him for two years and he was with his sons in the grocery store. But I'm not so sure you know why (haha!) I love him. You might think I love him because Daddy is dead and I loved Daddy and I'm trying to replace Daddy so I've fallen in love with an older man. You can think that if you want to. And maybe part of it is true. But that doesn't change anything. There are probably nine billion hidden psychological reasons that go back nine billion years as to why anybody falls in love with anybody. Have you ever seen penguins choose a mate? Thousands of them will be hanging out together on some big glacier and they all look the same, but for some microscopically subtle reasons, penguin no. 4,723 and penguin no. 2,867 will choose each other. So, you can come up with ninety-nine million reasons why this 54 kilo penguin is in love with the penguin who teaches her English class. But reasons or no reasons, I still love him. Why do I love him? Why do you like Christmas more than Easter? Why is Jupiter bigger than Venus? Why did Michael Jackson die? Why is the sky blue? Sure there are reasons. Tons of them. But they don't change how I feel…I love his eyes, his nose, the way he stands and moves. I love his mouth and what it says. I love his hands and what and how they touch. I love the way he treats people, especially Laura Winger. But probably the most important thing is that I love him because he's the only person in this wild wicked wonderful world that I can really talk to. About everything. About language, lizards, life, fried chicken, causality, toilet paper, the color green, bullshit, nature, gods, gangs, gazpacho, old people, young people, no people, purple people, death, Daddy, dinosaurs, dingbats, Mommy, Mrs. Fluckinger, nothing, news, never, and now…I want to see him…now!

I knew I loved him when we were sitting on the bench on Tom Sawyer Island watching his kids play. I felt him feeling. I felt like I was inside of him. He was sitting there watching the two kids he loved more than life itself and knowing all the while that the mother of the kids didn't love him then, would never love him later, and had probably never really loved him before. I watched his eyes watch his kids. I watched his lips close and his head think. I could see there was no blame or anger for his wife for not loving him. He didn't lament his situation. He took it for what it was…the fucking truth! So what do you do with the truth? You take it in your hands and head and try to mould it into the best thing possible. You know you're stuck. You're always stuck. We all wallow in the mud. But there is light, and fruit trees, and bits of beauty. You try to grab some. You know you will die, but before you die you will try to live the best you can. He stared at those kids knowing that one day the bubble would burst, one day they would know the truth about their parents, one day he and his wife would separate and they would try to spare those kids as much pain as possible. I felt him. And I felt him feeling me. He didn't try to touch me or seduce me. But I could feel that he loved me. Not like a daughter or a student. But as a human being. A woman with a body and mind. From the day in school when I knew he wasn't a pedantic pinhead (remember, that's what I called him), I always felt that he was feeling for me. Not just for me, but for all his students. But I was different…the transplanted American with the dead mother and the dying father, the girl who wrote what she thought and had a slew of questions about life and death and everything in between. He was thirty-nine. I was seventeen. I didn't think about love in the beginning. Slowly love thought about me…and him. Daddy died and I turned eighteen. His wife turned lesbian. I tried Johnny. I had already tried Cherif and Chuckie and Marcel Monney. I found out I didn't love any of them. I went to Paris with the Fluckingers. I watched Mommy and Daddy and the boys. Love started slowly crawling up my leg like a gentle spider. It built a nest on my heart. And now I love him. Should I not love him? And if he loves me, should we let the world prevent us from loving each other? I'm eighteen. The law is out of the way. No more messing with a minor to worry about. I'm not that fifteen-year-old English girl who ran away to France with her Math teacher…

Vacation is over. Yesterday when I saw him at school I knew I loved him. And when he looked at me, I was quite sure he loved me.

I don't know what I'm going to do. He's still my teacher for another nine months. Teachers and students aren't supposed to love each other. It's bad for business. Can't kiss. Can't lick. Can't even hold hands after class...

24

Natasha is sure she's pregnant. She's a mess. She can't sleep. She feels sick. She comes to school looking like she had walked twenty miles to get there. Of course she hasn't told her parents. In class today I compared her situation to what mine might have been in similar circumstances. If I had gone to Greece with Daddy and ended up screwing some guy on a beach the night before we flew back to Switzerland, what would he have said? How would he have reacted? I'm 99% sure that he would have been the nicest, most considerate man and said, *Well Laura, what are we going to do about this? Maybe you weren't too smart to drink all that ouzo and take a midnight stroll with Aristotle…but it's done. Come to think about it, I did a few dumb things in my younger days. I was just lucky I didn't get pregnant. For that, girls have it tougher than boys…So you don't know the guy's last name…You don't have his phone number or email address…We could go back to Santorini and try to find him…But did you love him? Do you want to try to find him? Do want to keep the baby? We've never really talked about abortion…How do you feel about it? It's a question I've never been sure about. I did have a girlfriend who had an abortion once…Actually I had two girlfriends who had abortions, but in one case I wasn't the father. She had gone away for the summer – we were in college – and got pregnant with another guy. Of course I was devastated because I thought we were in love…With the other girl I was the father…at least that's what she told me and I had no reason not to believe her. I was twenty-four and she was nineteen. I told her it was her choice. She said it was my choice too. We decided we didn't want to get married and she wanted a career before a kid. She got the abortion. I always felt bad about it. How does one know what's right and wrong?…So anyway, Laura, what do you want to do? What do you think is the right thing to do? I don't think Aristotle needs to know about it if you don't want him to know…*

I would have laughed when he kept calling the guy "Aristotle". But Natasha's parents won't make her laugh. She thinks they'll go ape shit. She thinks they'll yell and scream and they'll make her have the baby and go find Aristotle and make him marry her. She's eighteen. She doesn't want to get married or have a baby. They have their strict religious beliefs. It's a horrible situation. Horrible. Just horrible.

So who is right and who is wrong? Would Daddy's reaction have been "the right" reaction? Maybe Natasha's parents are right for believing in their god and good and evil and sin and that their daughter has sinned and now must pay the price and have the baby. The only thing Daddy might have been pissed off about is that I let Aristotle inside the treasure chest without "protection". He might have said, "Laura, how can you be that stupid?" And it would have been a very good question. But otherwise I don't think he would have turned it into a big moral issue like Natasha's parents will. But again, who the hell knows what the best way to raise a kid is? All I know is that she is going crazy and that some kids have committed suicide for less. I'm trying to think of a way out for her. Could she get an abortion without her parents knowing it? It might be possible. There's only one person I can think of who might be able to help…

Natasha, Laura called me last night and told me what has happened to you. I could tell this first week in class that you weren't your normal self. But I didn't know the gravity of the situation. I do need you to explain why you don't want to tell your parents about it.

They would kill me…maybe not kill me, but they would be so mad…I don't really know what they'd do…but I think they'd make me have the baby. They're totally against abortion. Their religion is against abortion. They follow their religion…

And you don't?

No, not really. I don't know who to follow.

Are you against abortion?

No…sometimes. I think every case is maybe different. If I knew the boy – guy – better and maybe loved him or something, then it might be different. But I knew him for three hours in a dumb discotheque.

Do you want to try to go find him? He's half responsible for your condition.

I don't want to find him. I don't want to blame him.

What happened is my fault.

Maybe "fault" is the wrong word. But you're both responsible.

But he's in Greece and I'm here. If I wanted to find him, I'd have to tell my parents. I couldn't take off back to Greece for a few days without them knowing about it.

Maybe you could think up another excuse.

I don't want to see him again. I don't want to get anyone else involved.

You're sure…

I just want this to be over with…

So you do want an abortion.

Yes.

And you've thought about it.

Yes, Mr. Fluck…

Natasha started crying. Up to this point it had surprised me how stoic she had been. I think she had prepared herself. But the emotion finally dripped out of her. Since Daddy's funeral I think crying is one of the best things you can do sometimes. I had brought Kleenex. I set them in front of her and put my hand on her shoulder for a few seconds. Mr. Fluckinger had thought I should be there, too. He let a good minute go by.

Natasha, what I can do for you is call a friend of mine who works at the hospital in Nyon. He's a wonderful person and I think he'll be able to help you.

Thank you…Mr….

You are eighteen, aren't you Natasha?

Ye…ye…yes.

My guess is that you could go in in the morning and be out in the afternoon...just like a school day...if you see what I mean.

Ye...yes...sir.

I must admit, I loved the "sir" that came out of her lovely trembling mouth. When Mr. Fluckinger suggested a call to his friend in Nyon, I suddenly felt the whole situation become much lighter. There was "a possibility". Sometimes just the possibility of a possibility is all one needs to put a little sunshine in a black sky.

Laura said you've been pregnant for about a month. Is that right?

Yes.

Then we had better get moving. I'll call my friend tonight and give you whatever news I have tomorrow afternoon.

Tha...thank...thank you Mr. Fluckinger.

Laura, do you have time to walk home with Natasha?

He looked at me, raised his eyebrows and nodded his head slightly.

Of course.

Okay. See you tomorrow.

25

For quite a while I've been seeing him in action in English class. I watched him be a father in Paris. This week I observed him as he threw a life buoy to a friend who was drowning in the wild ocean of late adolescence and pull her to some dry land. I love him. I won't go into all the details of what happened. But Natasha got the abortion and her parents never found out about it. The whole thing went amazingly smoothly. We took the six-forty-five train together to Nyon. By seven-thirty we were at the hospital. Mr. Fluckinger's friend met us at the entrance. We went up an elevator. I was shown into a waiting room and she went down a corridor with the doctor. She was back at eleven. We were in school at two.

I think Natasha was so relieved to have "a solution" to her problem, that she hardly seemed nervous on the way to the hospital. On the way back all she could talk about was how nice the doctors and nurses were and how she didn't feel a thing. She asked me if I had an idea of a present she could give to Mr. Fluckinger.

It was definitely a happy ending to what could have been a very ugly mess. This kind of thing can destroy some people. Fortunately Natasha came out in one piece. In fact, I think she grew from it. As I watched her looking out of the window in the train on the way home, I saw a girl I had never seen before. Normally she would have been talking to me, listening to music, and looking at all the boys who walked by – all at once! Here she actually appeared calm, almost beatific, and every now and then she'd say something like, *I never thought it would be over…or…isn't the world amazing…or…life looks different now…*

Shit happens. Some messes get cleaned up, others get more shit thrown on top. Mr. Fluckinger and his friend saved the day. If anything delicious or disastrous ever happens between him and me somewhere down life's long and winding road, at least now there is probably somebody out there I can talk to about it. My guess is that Natasha is a real friend.

26

I can't believe I watched the first presidential debate. I didn't plan to, but I woke up in the middle of the night, looked at the clock, and I remembered 3am Swiss time was 8pm Denver time and the opening gong of light-heavyweight championship bout between Romney and Obama was just ready to sound. So I got out of bed and turned on the TV. I think if I still lived in America I wouldn't care about politics very much, but living over here changes everything. People are always asking me questions – mostly dumb ones like "How could anybody vote for a Mormon millionaire?" or "How could you not vote for Obama?" – so for whatever reason, I've taken to following the circus. I guess it's also simple nostalgia. It all reminds me of "home", my California roots, the country where the seed called Laura Winger got planted and grew into a ten-year-old palm tree until her Daddy pulled it out of the ground and transplanted it to a nice little country in the middle of Europe. Here in Switzerland people have so many different roots and have come for so many different reasons. In my class there are students from Portugal, Spain, Italy, Kosovo, Bosnia, France, the Congo, Malaysia, Vietnam, and of course Natasha who's a mix of everything. Some families come for work, others are refugees of wars or nasty political systems, some are just rich people who want to

138

settle in a stable place with great scenery and relative security. If you think about it for five seconds, every person on earth is a massive mixed salad because every person has two parents who had two parents who had two parents who had two parents and it all goes back to the beginning of time which probably had no beginning. (I read a quote the other day..."Time is man's most original invention"...I like that...) Nobody wants to think about all this because it's a lot easier just to take the roots where you're born and suck on them for the rest of your life and say, "I'm American" or "I'm Swiss" or "I'm East Mongolian". It's kind of sad when you think about it because it keeps the world from uniting, but maybe the world was never meant to unite. Maybe sucking on nationalistic roots is just an extension of sucking your thumb or sucking the corner of your favorite blanket or the ear of your teddy bear. Maybe people need to suck on what they're closest to – first it's a mommy's breast, then it's a country... But I am glad that Daddy brought me over here because now I have TWO ROOTS. Maybe one day I'll run away to South Korea and live in a cave or a tree house with Mr. Fluckinger and then I'll have THREE ROOTS. I guess fanatics are people who think the whole world should suck on their roots and if they don't suck on their roots they are "evil" or "sinful" or "wicked" and should be either cured, converted, kicked out, or killed. Actually that's what I don't like about America: so many "Americans" (whose ancestors were all born in Europe or Africa or wherever) have never seen any other part of the world, yet they go around blowing their horns and saying it's the greatest country on earth. That's like eating only fried chicken your whole life and saying fried chicken is the world's best food! Not too bright sometimes, hey America... But back to the boxing match...

Mitt kicked Barack's shiny butt. And he did it with a smile on his face. Barack's teethy smile looked fake. Everybody says Romney's a plastic fake. Here Obama looked like the imposter. Maybe he just had a bad day, but he looked like he was just acting a part in a play and his role was to bullshit enough people to keep his job as President of the Yooo-nited States of America. Maybe Romney was acting too. But he actually gave the impression (at least he gave me the impression) that he wanted the job to help the people of the Yooo-nited States of America have better lives. Obama gave the impression he was trying to help Obama keep that nice big white house on Pennsylvania Avenue in Washington D.C. I'm sure Obama will make a comeback in the next debate. But the more I thought about the whole thing, the more I wondered what percentage of the world's politicians are really in the business to help their country or state or city – or world for that matter – and how many are in it to HELP THEMSELVES. Maybe it's possible to do both at the same time...One thing's sure: nobody's in politics to HURT THEMSELVES. I guess it all comes back to something Daddy and I used to talk about: is it possible to do an UNegotistical act. Even when you're trying to help somebody – like Mr. Fluckinger and I were doing with Natasha – are you just helping the person because if you DON'T HELP THE PERSON you will feel worse than if you DO HELP THE PERSON? It's probably another one of those questions we'll never know the answer to. Maybe the only thing that really matters is that SOMEBODY helps the Natashas of the world. Even then, how do we know we're really helping? Maybe we helped Natasha commit a great SIN by killing the one-month-old fetus in her belly. That's what the right-wingers would say anyway. The laura-wingers would say they just tried to help a friend with a problem. The left-wingers might say Natasha should stop spending her money on clothes and iPods and start giving it to the poor. The right-wingers might say giving money to the poor doesn't help them; you have to give them jobs. The laura-wingers would wonder if in the end anybody really knows or cares what's right or wrong or good or bad…and anyway, win or lose, Obama and Romney are both cute and rich and have nice wives and families and plenty of cookies in their cookie jars…

Back to my beautiful hand-carved ego. The man I dream about asked me after class today if I had watched the debate. So we – Mr. Bernard Fluckinger and I – stood next to his desk and had a great conversation about all the stuff I just wrote about. English is my last class of the day on Thursday and my class is his last class which means that neither of us had to go anywhere after the bell rang and all the other kids had grabbed their books and coats and hightailed it out of the room. The fact that he stopped me as I was slowly meandering toward the door meant one thing...that he wanted to spend a bit more time with me. How much time? Only time will tell. But this time the time we spent talking at his desk was just long enough for both of us to feel that it wasn't enough time. It went something like this:

Obama really didn't look like his normal self.

Maybe people are getting a little tired of his normal self. People do get tired of each other. It's human nature I guess. The nature of nature...change. That might make a good subject for a composition one day.

I had this funny impression that he was only out for himself.

That would be another good topic.

The next debate will be interesting at least.

Yeah, the whole world will want to see if King Obama bounces back...

And if Romney makes one of his dumb mistakes...He surely didn't look dumb last night.

Good for him. He's taken a lot of shit lately...By the way, how is Natasha getting along?

Really well.

In class she seems like a totally different person.

I think the whole mess made her think about things. She matured a couple of years in a month.

Well, maybe it was all for the better.

Thanks to you and your friend.

All I did was make a phone call to a friend. All he did was do what doctors do.

Neither of us said anything for a few seconds. The clock ticked. My heart ticked. Mr. Fluckinger started putting things in his briefcase.

Well Laura, happy endings are better than sad endings.

I smiled coyly.

I guess everything has an ending.

If that's the case then everything also has a beginning...

We walked to the door. He pushed the handle and held it open for me. I slid past him into the hall brushing the back of his hand with my elbow.

O help me Dear Almighty God and Lord and Creator and Savior of this Earth and all the Galaxies large and small, large like the Milky Way and small like Ant Hills. Please All-Powerful Divinity, please help me to get through this Life without making too big of a Mess of Things. Bless me and Everybody Else on this Earth and in the rest of the Universe (in case there are other Earths with Creatures), bless Us All that We might find some Love in this Life, some Reason to carry Us from Day to Day, from Cradle to Casket or Ashes, some Reason to make Us want to get out of Bed every Day and praise Life and rejoice that there is Something and not Nothing, some Reason to make Us want to turn off the fucking TV and go for a Walk in the Rain and meet our Lover and best Friend, or even be alone but not forever alone because it has been proven over and over that Human Beings need other Human Beings. Please, bless Us all that the Holes in our Hearts with be filled with enough Love that We won't perish and die some useless Death in some desolate Corner of Nowhere where loveless rotten Angels reign. Amen.

That's all I could think of as I was walking home. I can see how praying could be fun. Thinking and writing are a lot like praying. Fairy tales swooping in and out of the brain. Praying that there's a god, a love, a world, a yesterday, a tomorrow…

I forgot to pray about whether or not abortion is wrong. I also forgot to ask if falling in love with your teacher is wrong. Is any love wrong? Does any love ever turn out right? People say abortion is wrong because you're killing a fetus. Nobody seems to care about all the sperms that die trying to get into that egg. Millions of them every time. They all die without reaching their goal. Don't they count for anything? Sperms, worms, germs. But they're not human beings, you say. Why are human beings the measure of all things? Don't birds think they are the measure of all things? Don't flowers and trees and cats and lizards and English teachers and Obamas and Romneys and parentless girls and moons and stars and Hell's Angels and Taliban terrorists think they are the measure of all things? Doesn't every single solitary creature…?

Will it all blow up one day?

Will it all disappear?

Will it never disappear?

Will it keep humming its quiet hum like an old refrigerator?

Good night Laura.

Who else can I say good night to?

God?

Okay.

Good Night God.

I wonder who first invented the idea of god. It must have been very cold outside. The creature must have been freezing toward death. Or maybe a little girl was searching in a forest for her lost rabbit. Or could it have been unbelievable joy – or love – that had a creature raising its arms in exaltation and thanking…God?

27

The earth is turning and circling. It's now called October. In Switzerland we get a two-week vacation from school. An autumn break to look at the leaves changing color and falling. I've changed color. I dyed my hair a reddish brown. It's normally kind of a dark brown. Mr. Fluckinger likes it. He told me so the other day. He was the only teacher who noticed I had changed it. At least he was the only one who mentioned it.

laura   you changed your hair

yeah   it s autumn

good idea   be part of the flow of nature

mr fluckinger   do you ever think about how horrible nature is

of course   every day   every day of my life

me too

and i think of how wonderful it is too   it s horrible and wonderful at the same time

all the leaves on all the trees fall off and rot

but first they were beautiful

i guess so

what are you doing for the vacation

you mean am i going anywhere

that   whatever

i kind of forget to plan ahead   i feel like i m always on vacation   school is vacation   i get to come here and see

146

you

> *and i get to see you*

He knew. I knew.

> *what about you and your family*
> *we re staying here   my wife works   i might take the*
boys to the zoo in servion   why don t you come along
> *i d love too*
> *when*
> *monday*
> *would your wife care*
> *of course not   you re our babysitter and she s in love*
with another woman   she did ask me the other night if i
had ever had an affair with a student
> *what did you say*
> *no*

The advantage of having school is that it occupies my brain. My brain is a kite and school is the string. It keeps me close to the ground. But at the same time I always feel like I'm on another planet. I try to listen to people – students, teachers – but most of the time I feel like I'm on the outside of the conversation. Like they're talking a foreign language. Except with Mr. Fluckinger of course.

> *so i ll pick you up monday at about eleven*
> *okay great   the last time i was there was with my father*
and cherif

who s cherif

he was kind of my first boyfriend   i guess he was my first real boyfriend but when we were at the zoo i realized we were very different   i remember it like it was yesterday

you mean the cherif who plays rugby

yes how did you know

he's my student too

i didn t know that

yeah he s a really good kid   very polite and attentive

i hardly ever talk to him anymore

the world turns

and brings on the seasons   one after another   i love the seasons

me too   all of them   that's one reason i love switzerland

when we were at the zoo   my father and i were looking at all the unbelievable creatures and thinking how life was an insane miracle   all cherif could think about was putting his hand on my derrière

boys will be boys

yeah   but in the end we just didn t share enough   since my father died   a lot of times i feel like there s really no one   no one to talk to   except you i guess   i ve been thinking   i ve been asking myself   why do i have to live in this world   and i think i don t   i don t that s all

what do you mean

i mean why can t i   or we   or anybody   just forget about this world   ignore it   yeah that s a better word and create our own world   kind of like walt disney did

with disneyland   he tried to take all the ugliness out of the
world   he created his magic kingdom   i m not saying
my world would be all roses and cream   but at least it
wouldn t be full of so much bullshit   we spend our whole
lives ignoring what s going on in places like antartica and
greenland   when you think about it we ignore ninety-nine
percent of everything that's going on in the world   so
i just want to ignore the other one percent   the one percent
around me   the bullshit   i can create my own world
     it might be kind of lonely on your planet   but i like
the idea
     can't be much lonelier than it already is
     you know what i ve been thinking about lately
     no what
     i ve been wondering which is worse   to spend your life
believing in god or spending your life believing in man
maybe the worst is to spend your life believing in both
god can t save the world and man can t save the world   the
whole idea of saving the world is ridiculous   yet i ve been
obsessed with it all my life   i should just forget about it
stop thinking about it   accept the horrors and the injustice
and the inequality and stop thinking that anybody is going
to clean up the mess   i m kind of agreeing with your idea
     none of us have much time left   how many days
years   seasons are left for anybody   i just want to stop
wallowing around in the bullshit
     what a world
     it s like a coloring book   we might as well color it with
the colors we like

*it s also like teaching   a teacher can teach pretty much
however he wants   if he wants to be a hard ass and give
everybody bad notes he can   if he wants to help kids he can
if he wants to punish kids he can   if he wants to make it
all amusing he can   if he wants to be boring as hell he
can   any two teachers can teach the same subject in two
totally different ways so it ends up not even being the same
subject   if you see what i mean*

sure   so my idea is to do the same thing with my life

let s start by taking it to the zoo on monday

okay

so is eleven o clock okay

i ll be in front of my house   you know where it is

yes   boulevard de grancy across from the supermarket

have a good weekend

for some reason i m not real fond of weekends

me neither actually

28

I finally figured out what the hell I'm doing. I'm writing two books about the two most important subjects in this world. My first book, "Don't Bullshit Me Daddy", was about death. This one is about love. Death and love. Nobody wants to die and everybody wants to love and be loved. I guess you can't really say nobody wants to die because people kill themselves all the time and lots of seriously suffering people often say they've had enough life to last a lifetime and want to get off the stage. Does everybody want to love and be loved? That's probably not true either because so many people are so full of hate that love is off life's menu. But for me, now, love and death are number one and two on life's hit parade. Mommy died. Daddy died. There is death all around us every minute of every day. I learned early. I can't get it out of my head. When death is so real, life becomes very real, too. This is it…"life"…this is all we have…So how are we going to live it? – I'm lucky (unlucky?). I don't have to worry about money and a job. Daddy left me enough money to get me through the century. So I have even more time to fill up than most people do. How do I fill it up? What counts for little Laura Winger? What do I decide to do with my seconds, minutes, hours, days, and years on this lovely little planet?

Something tells me that what counts the most is having someone to share the world with. I'm writing this book to "share"...share what? What I think...what I feel...how I see and experience the whole big bag of tomatoes. Share with whom? I shared the world with Daddy. Daddy dead. I tried to share it with Cherif. Love dead. That was Book One....And now this is Book Two.

You know, you can only share when you feel similar things and see the world in similar ways. And that's where love comes from. At least that's where it starts. Sharing. Feeling. Go to the zoo with somebody you think you might love. There you can really see if you share the same view of the world. I went with Cherif. He'd just say things like "Oh, look at the tiger"...or..."Oh, there's a flamingo". He just put names on things. But names don't tell you one single solitary thing about anything. Giving something a name tells you nothing about what the thing is. Cherif also wanted to put his hand on my butt all the time. I wanted to put my hand on his butt, too. But I also wanted to share the world with him. The hand on the butt feels a lot better if the hand and the butt share a certain feeling about what hands and butts are...about what being alive is...about everything alive...tigers, flamingos, ducks, goats, clouds, mice, foxes, men, women, grass, flowers, trees, water, rain...the whole zoo...THE WHOLE DAMN ZOO. I guess that's why people usually marry somebody of the same religion, because they have the same god that gives the same answers to all the same questions. But I don't have a religion. I need somebody with whom I can create questions and poke around in the desert for answers or no answers. At the zoo Mr. Fluckinger said to me, "You know, Laura, the deeper you dig, the bigger the hole gets." Can we dig a hole together…?

29

But this is much more than a love story. It's not some 10-cent girl-falls-in-love-with-her-teacher trashy tale. This is a "life" story. Dickens wrote "A Tale of Two Cities". This is "A Tale of Two Lives", two lives coming together, slowly entwining to form one very strong rope.

This story has nothing to do with right or wrong, good or evil, morality or immorality, prurience or innocence. It's not about whether or not Bernard Fluckinger should or should not have laced his fingers into Laura Winger's when she extended her hand across the table on the terrace of the restaurant at the Servion Zoo. There is no should or shouldn't. There is only he did or didn't.

This story has everything to do with two creatures who were born in two different corners of the universe and whose paths happened to cross thanks to an infinity of circumstances and who were pulled to each other like an apple falling in slow-motion to a certain singular spot on the ground.

Most people like to think that things happen "for a reason". Neither Bernard Fluckinger nor I think that anything happens for "a reason". He doesn't think he married a lesbian for "a reason". He doesn't think that John Lennon was assassinated for "a reason". He doesn't think the tsunami that killed a quarter of a million people in Asia happened for "a reason". I don't think I was born for "a reason". I don't think my mother died of some insane blood cancer for "a reason". I don't think I ended up in Mr. Fluckinger's English class for "a reason".

Nothing happens for a reason. But everything happens for an infinity of reasons – an infinite web of events that are all linked together and can never be understood by the human head. It's a waste of time to think, "Why did this or that happen?" The only question is, "What do we do now?" Where do we go from here? Do we keep on loving or do we say we can't do this?

We had walked through the whole zoo. We had looked at all the animals, including each other. Ozzie and Freddie were playing in the playground next to the terrace of the restaurant. There are swings, slides, and teeter-totters and various things to climb on. Bernie and I were alone on the terrace except for an elderly couple that were making goo-goo eyes at a child in a stroller. I was drinking tea and he was having a beer. The weather was nice. There was a slight breeze and yellow leaves fell intermittently from the birch trees behind the playground. I can't remember what we were talking about. The boys were running and jumping like the monkeys we had just seen. Bernie's left arm was slightly extended and the fingers were resting on the stem of his beer glass. We both saw my right hand set the teacup down and glide across the table and settle on his fingers. For a moment his hand and eyes didn't move, then the parts slowly softly locked.

For whatever reason I woke up at three o'clock in the morning. I remembered the boxing match was on, live from the state of New York. It's still October vacation. I didn't have to get up in the morning. There was nothing I had to do today except stay alive and maybe write. I got out of bed and sleep-walked to the living room. I pulled a blanket over my naked legs and turned on the TV. There they were, already duking it out. Obama in the red tie, Romney in the blue tie. Obama was trying to be tough because all the critics said he wasn't tough enough in the first debate. Every chance he got he smacked Romney below the belt or pulled out his trusty six-shooter and fired a few blanks. Romney ducked and dodged and tried to say what a lousy president Obama had been. Again I thought Obama was just acting. Romney seemed more sincere, but that doesn't mean he'd be a better president. Two things stuck in my little head. First, Obama often didn't answer the question he was asked. He went to his canned speeches about Romney paying less taxes than nurses or garbage collectors and how his – Obama's - mom had been a single-family mom or his grandpa had fought in World War II, whatever that has to do with anything…Anyway, the whole thing was some kind of a huge joke. Farce is a better word. Actually what got me most was when a nice lady in the crowd very politely asked the candidates what they were going to do about all the guns that were killing so many people in the streets of America. Guns…What are you going to do about all the guns, gentlemen? The answer: NOTHING. Both candidates just babbled about enforcing the laws that already exist. Neither candidate said one single solitary word about making these guns illegal to own or illegal to carry around. What I want to know is: Why didn't one of them have the gonads to look the world in the eye and say, "We are supposed to be a nation founded on Christian principles. Christianity – last I heard – is supposed to be based on the life of a guy named Jesus Christ…good ol' Jee-Jee Christ. So let me ask you this: Would Jesus have owned a gun? Would Jesus have carried a gun around in his toga pocket? Never! Never! Never! And you damn well know it! Would Jesus want his disciples to tote guns? Of course not! Did Jesus's Father, the Great God Amighty, inspire the Second Amendment? Of course nobody knows, but I surely doubt it. Did circumstances in America in 1776 inspire the Second Amendment? Of course they did…Absolutely! So let's get real people. Neither God nor His Son had anything to do with allowing Americans to buy and carry lethal weapons that can kill in an instant. It was the world in 1776. But friends, it's a different world today. Drugs that used to be legal are illegal today. Guns should go the same route. Driving too fast on America's roads is illegal because it's dangerous. Guns should be illegal because they're dangerous. Some of you say, But guns are fun to shoot for sport. Driving a car too fast can also be fun. Drive your cars fast on race tracks and shoot your guns only at shooting ranges. Make them illegal everywhere else. Everywhere! But we need guns to protect ourselves! Aren't far more people killed than protected?....Of course, ladies and gentlemen of this great nation, the problem is much deeper than just the guns. Of course it's about gun lobbies and gun makers who want to cram more and more money into their already bulging pockets. Of course much of the problem comes from the horrible ghettos – ghettos that are the result of a nation that started with European people buying and selling African people. And of course our lousy schools need to be fixed. Of course we have screwed up in the Middle East and Afghanistan. But let's at least clean up our house. Let's stop putting guns in people's hands in America. And let's do it now! Right now! How many more people need to be murdered before we, as a nation – as an intelligent populace – ban all these mother fucking guns?"...

I'm sorry. I couldn't help myself. But I get carried away. And the whole mess reminds me of Daddy. "Guns" was one of the few subjects that got up his gander. Of course neither Obama nor Romney could say this. Because if they did they'd lose votes. That's the whole problem. Politicians today aren't leading; they're following. That's why the stupid boat just keeps floating down the same stupid stream. There's no pilot to turn it around, to get it to change course. The politicians just try to please the masses and the masses are stupid. There is so much stupid shit out there. Can we blame Obama and Romney? Not really. They're just trying to win a dumb boxing match.

31

laura you re nice to people   i watch you   you re always good to the other kids in the class

there s no reason not to be   none of them asked to be born   they can t help being who they are   the world s bad enough as it is   there s no need to make it worse

is that how your father thought

yes   as he got older he started to lose a little patience with people   but he was still nice to them   he used to say that you have two choices: either you kill the fly that is circling around your head or you let it be a fly and let it do what flies do   he always chose the latter   he couldn't kill a fly   aren t you the same way

pretty much so   you can t turn a fly into a flower

but you can turn it into a dead fly   you try to help all the kids too

what else are teachers for

i think a lot of teachers don t know what they re for   or they don t take the time to think about what they re really doing   about what they re trying to put into our cute little heads and what is the best way to go about doing it

i don t get into other teachers business

did you see the debate

i watched a little on youtube

what did you think

obama s magic is definitely starting to wear off   i think people are beginning to get tired of him   not so much here in europe because we don t see that much of him   but i read the american press and even the liberals are starting to throw darts at him

have you ever been to america   i ve never asked you before

i went to high school one year when i was eighteen

where were you

in new mexico

really   did you like it

school was ridiculously easy   i got straight A s without even trying   most of the kids were nice   i lived with a family that had a kid my age   we had nothing in common it s all kind of a blur now   it s amazing how much i don t remember

what do you remember

the feeling of being in one of those yellow school buses full of kids and looking out of the window and feeling alone i always felt alone   but i didn't mind it   i think it was good for me   at first it is was difficult but i got used to it i remember autumn   more than anything else   the american football games   the cheerleaders and pompom girls   the weather getting cooler   the desert changing color

We were in a tea-room across the street from my apartment. Every now and then our legs rubbed. Our eyes constantly rubbed. Isn't that a way to know when you're really in love?

how did you feel when you first came to switzerland

i was ten you know daddy and i learned french together
after a few months in school i spoke the language and didn
t feel like a foreigner anymore   i used to watch a lot of
tv just to hear french

do you ever think of going back to america

you know i haven t been back since i came here   daddy
and i never went back   it s been eight years   i think he
just didn't want to face the memories of my mother s death
he wanted to keep me at a distance from it all   we never
really even talked about going back

it s a nice place

there are a lot of nice places in the world

i guess any place can be heaven and any place can be
hell   it depends on what you make of it

and who you re with   why did you decide to be a
teacher

i never decided to be a teacher   it just sort of happened
like most things   when i was a student at the university
i did substitute teaching to make some money   i enjoyed
the kids   one thing led to another

what made you want to get married

i d say that just kind of happened too   i was there
she was there   i was thirty and tired of messing around
she was twenty eight and probably bi sexual but didn't tell
me about it   i think she wanted to have a go at having
kids   she had her go   now she wants to go somewhere
else   i surely won't try to stop her

would she leave the kids

There's not one thing I don't like about Mr. Fluckinger. Nothing. I like it all. The way he talks, walks, dresses, smiles, treats waitresses in tea-rooms, sees the world, the shape of the head, colors, clothes, wrists, fingers, ears, eyes, cheeks. That's just the way it is. He says the same about me.

32

It's been three weeks since Natasha had her abortion. I wonder how I would have felt if it had been me. Would I have kept the baby? Would it have depended on who the daddy was?

She called this morning. She's in love. She had to tell somebody. She's in love with a guy named Johnny. Yeah, that Johnny. Who better to tell than me?

She bumped into him yesterday walking across the Place St. François. They made eye contact, slowed down, stopped, talked, went to Starbucks for a cup of coffee, and boom, wham, zap, click, zowie…She couldn't stop talking. I did my best to listen.

Doesn't everybody need somebody to talk to? But the question is not just who can you talk to, but also what can you say that might have a chance of being understood? That's the hitch…I haven't told anybody about Bernie and me because I don't know if I know anybody who would understand. Our love is not on the map. It's hard to find people to talk to about places that aren't not the map.

Actually, I always thought Johnny and Natasha would make a good couple…whatever that means. They both kind of like the same things. They kind of walk the same walk and talk the same talk. According to her, it was love at first sip. They spent two hours together in Starbucks.

Evidently, first they talked about me:

hey, things happen   maybe we weren t right for each other   laura s a special kind of person   she s been through a lot   she might need a special kind of love anyway i didn t have what she wanted   but that s okay   i ve moved on   i really did like her though

you know she s probably my best friend   we ve been though a lot together   she liked you a lot johnny   i don t know what it was   maybe she wasn t ready for a relationship so soon after her father died

i don t know   she s different   i really can t say why it didn't work

the truth is without her   without her and my English teacher   i don't know where i d be today

what do you mean

it s something i haven t told anybody about   i don t think she has either   i guess i can tell you johnny   i mean since everything is okay now   but you have to have to promise me you won't tell anybody

of course not

i was in greece at the end of the summer with my parents and……

I can't believe she told Johnny about the abortion. Yes I can. She wanted to get close to him. I did too. But what I would tell him, he didn't seem to hear the way I said it. That was the problem. Evidently, he heard her the way she wanted to be heard. She said, "Oh Laura, I felt like I could talk to him about anything…absolutely anything."

I thought, "That, friends, might be the secret to love." At least that's the way I feel with Bernie. And that's not the way I felt with Cherif, Marcel Monney, Chuckie, and Johnny.

Natasha has somebody to love. So much the better. She's excited. I'm happy for her. I'm sure Johnny will call one day and tell me about it too. But I won't tell Natasha or Johnny about my love. Not now. Not yet. I'll just write about it. The Laura Winger Story. The no bullshit story. The story that keeps me company when I can't be with the man I love.

And my story is nearing the end. After Natasha called, Bernie came over. We made love for the first time. I've lived long enough to know that making love and having sex are two very different things. I had had sex quite a few times in my life. This morning was the first time I made love.

33

Vacation's over. We're back in school. You're wondering how it feels to sit in class and listen to the man I love teach. It's kind of fun actually. He always laughs at the word "teach". "Teach what?" he says. "I have no idea how what I say will get chewed up and digested in another mind. Nobody really teaches. You throw out pieces of meat. Sometimes the scavengers are hungry, but usually they're not." Well, I'm hungry. But he's hungry too. I listen to him and he listens to me. We just have private sessions to supplement the group lessons. He came over three times last week. Twice at noon. Once after school. As far as I can tell, we're teaching each other what it feels like to really love and be loved. So far all the pieces fit. So far that great puzzle called "amour" is getting put together with the most delicate eyes and fingers. Of course it's all being done with the greatest discretion. We have to keep the door locked. But when you think about it, everything in life happens behind closed doors. Behind the closed doors of the human head. Behind the eyes, nose, ears, mouth, and skin. Everything happens back there, within. Within what? What are my insides? Is a human body a closed system? Is it self-contained? Maybe my insides are my outsides? Maybe my head records everything then spits it all back at the world. How close can you get to another person?

How close can you get to yourself? Does getting close to another person allow you to get closer to yourself? That's how it felt with Daddy. But the closer I got to Johnny the further away I felt from myself. What is "myself"? I'm always "myself". How can I not be myself. So what does that all mean? I guess it means that loving someone is being comfortable with the person, sharing, taking the world apart and putting it back together again. With Johnny, when things started to come loose, they stayed loose. With Daddy, things would get tighter...So how much of me is Daddy? Who cares? I am what I am...

Bernie and I seem to share everything. It's been that way from the beginning, from the first time he talked to me after school about my Hemingway paper. We can talk about anything. We can laugh and be serious at the same time about the same subject. When we're together the clock doesn't tick. The hands of the clock go round and round all crazily like...Alice in Wonderland...Time flies. Time doesn't exist. Sometimes when we make love it feels like it was for hours. But it was only for a few minutes. Sometimes it's the opposite. It's the same with talking. Sometimes I feel like Bernie's growing inside me and I'm growing inside him. I didn't know it was possible. Not like this. He didn't either. When we're together we both feel naked, even when we have our clothes on. It's as if our skins are rubbing each other all the time. Like we're slowly becoming one skin. Of course it's early. The gates of Eden just opened. Will there be apples, snakes, and Gods mixing with the flowers? Will we get zapped by a thunderbolt? Will we write our own Bible?

In school we've started reading a new book, "The Stories of John Cheever". Bernie says we're probably the only group of gymnase students in Swiss school history to read John Cheever. Cheever used to write a lot in the New Yorker magazine. His novels were never very popular but his short stories were. But he wrote in the sixties and seventies and today you never see his name out there anymore. Not like Hemingway or Steinbeck. Cheever faded with the times and death. But Bernie loves his writing. He gave a little introductory speech today and said that Cheever's stories are very subtle – almost bleak – about rich people on the East Coast of America, and how most of them are like Madame Bovary. They never seem fulfilled. They all seem caught in a web of circumstances that keeps them from finding and sharing a deep love of life and happiness. And Cheever was a closet bisexual with a wife and kids. Bernie said he writes beautiful sentences and that a sentence can be as beautiful as a face or a flower. He said we would read a couple of stories and see how we liked them. He wasn't going to ram them down our throats. I just read "The Swimmer". A man is at a summer party a few miles from his house in a wealthy suburban neighborhood. He is a bit bored and a little drunk. He suddenly decides to "swim" home. He will swim across every private and public pool that he knows between where he is and his house. At first he is exhilarated and feels like an explorer walking through uncharted land wearing only a bathing suit. Little by little this feeling changes to fatigue, sadness and solitude. When he finally gets home his house is dark and empty.

Bernie and I don't want our house to be dark and empty. I wonder how long the feeling we have for each other can last...It feels like it can last forever. We had known each other a long time before we finally made love. Making love was the most natural extension of everything we had talked about and experienced together. We look through the same telescope. We look through the same microscope. When we finally put our lips together it felt like we were one mouth. When our bodies linked we were one body. Am I fooling myself? Is he fooling himself? Can a teacher and a student really "share" the world? Can they really "love" each other? Will the world let them love each other? Can Bernie and I somehow live "outside" this world we're planted in? Nobody knows. And nobody knows how the human mind works. Nobody knows why anybody does what they do. We like to think we do, but when you really get down and think about it, it's all way way too complicated. And like Daddy used to say, "Can a mind know itself? Can it know what's doing the knowing?" Am I crazy? Maybe. Are we all crazy? Probably. But do I have to be crazy like other people are crazy? Do I have to share their values and beliefs? Do I have to buy into the garbage they buy? Do I have to believe in the same gods? Do I have to watch the same movies, talk the same talk, read the same books and magazines? No, I don't. Are there lots of people out there like me? I'm sure there are. They're just hard to find. I found one and I love him. His name is Bernard Fluckinger and he happens to be my English teacher. How far will we go down the road of love? Will we get hit head on by an oncoming truck? Will the morality police pick us up? Will the car break down? How long will we have to keep it all a secret? Will we run out of gas before anybody finds out?

34

The last round between the two light-heavyweight contenders for Champion of the World was on TV last night. The judges say Obama won. I think the judges are full of crap. Obama didn't win. Romney didn't lose. Everybody lost. Sure, Obama was the best bullshitter. He threw the most "tough-guy" punches at Romney. But throwing tough-guy punches has nothing to do with winning a debate. Not the debate to be the most powerful man on earth. To win that debate you have to show that you are sincere and that you have concrete ideas about solutions for whatever problems you think can be solved. If a problem is unsolvable you should admit it. If the monster is out of control and can't be slowed down, admit it. I had the impression that both Romney and Obama were both play-acting. Romney was trying to look presidential. Obama was trying to show people how tough he was. But as for ideas, as for honest frank discussion, as for real solutions to real problems…I thought both candidates were full of donkey and elephant shit, both were just tossing peanuts to all the monkeys in the zoo. One thing is certain: they weren't making the monkeys more intelligent with logical arguments about big problems. I thought Romney was more sincere. He came off as at least wanting to make America a better place by finding ways to create a better economy. Obama seemed like he was only interested in keeping his job and keeping the Big White House for his home. Maybe I'm out in left field. But that's the way I saw it. No winner. Only losers. Everybody.

I'm tired. The debate came on at three in the morning and my first period I had a French test. French is really hard. Much harder than English. But I guess learning a million grammar details and exceptions is good training for the mind. Oh yeah? Why? Tell me why, Laura…Well, now that I think about it, I'm really not sure why…Oh, come on, Laura. How can you not be sure?…I don't know. Sometimes things just pop into my head and pop out of my mouth. I don't always know why I say what I say. Learning a million grammar rules has to be good for something, doesn't it? Why else would we have to learn them?…Do you think everything you learn in school is good for something?…Of course not. Most things I forget two minutes after the test…But doesn't school teach you to think?…No, most teachers don't teach anything about how to think…That's odd…That's just the way it is…It reminds me of the three Romney-Obama debates…

35

Hi Laura. This is Johnny.

Oh, hi Johnny. I was hoping you'd call. Natasha's been giving me the play-by-play.

I hope she spares you some of the details.

It's hard for me to know. But I'm really happy for both of you. She's been through a lot. She's really a great person.

She told me how much you helped her…you and your English teacher.

Yeah, he set up the whole abortion thing. All I did was go to the hospital with her.

Well, she says you supported her all the way.

What are friends for?

Laura…that's kind of why I'm calling.

What do you mean?

As a friend.

Of course you're my friend.

No, I mean as a friend wanting to help a friend.

Why do I need help? I'm not pregnant. I get good grades in school. My teachers like me…I think. I've got food and clothes and a few friends… like y…

Laura, listen…

Okay…I'm listening…

You know what I'm talking about.

Are you sure? I'm not sure…

Laura, I just want you to know that you need to be careful.

About what? Not drowning in the bathtub?

People are talking.

People always talk. It's the planetary sport…

Laura, they're talking about you and your English teacher.

Is that the same teacher that helped your girlfriend with her unwanted pregnancy problem?

You know what I'm talking about Laura.

People have seen him go into your apartment building.

Who are "people"?

Kids at school. Natasha's told me, but she said she didn't dare talk to you about it. I'm only calling to tell you to be careful.

What makes you or anybody else think that if my English teacher goes into the building where I live, that he's coming to see me? There are seven other apartments in here.

Laura, you might not know it, but since your father died people talk a lot about you. There aren't too many eighteen-year-olds who live alone in a big apartment on the Boulevard de Grancy and who probably have enough money in the bank to live forever.

Do you believe in forever, Johnny?

It depends on what day it is. But that's not what we're talking about.

You're the one who brought it up.

Laura, look. I'm only telling you this for your own good.

And for your teacher's own good. He's the one who stands to lose everything.

What do you mean by "everything"?

You know what I mean. His job. His career. His wife. His family. If it all gets out in the news…

Johnny, not one human being, dog, cat or mouse knows anything about what goes on if and when Mr. Fluckinger comes into my apartment.

I'm just telling you, Laura. People know he's not going to see you to give you private English lessons.

Maybe I'm giving him lessons.

Laura, it's your life…and his. I know I can't tell you what to do with it. I'm just warning you that you need to be careful.

Thanks Johnny. I appreciate it. And I appreciate the fact that you got right to the point and cut the bullshit.

You know I wouldn't bullshit you, Laura. I have too much respect for you.

And vice versa.

Thanks Johnny. Listen, I've got to go.

Okay.

Good to talk to you.

Bye.

I told Johnny I had to go. I didn't have to go anywhere. When was the last time I had to go anywhere? Daddy's funeral? The dentist? School? The hospital with Natasha? I don't have to go to any of those places. Who says I do? The fact is I almost didn't go to Daddy's funeral. I don't think I ever told you about it. It was both the most beautiful thing and the ugliest thing I've ever seen. If I see a dead cat on the side of the road, it makes me crazy. And that's a cat I've never known for one second in my life. Imagine how I felt at Daddy's funeral. In any case, there was no way I could have looked at his face. Not dead. But he didn't have a face anymore. He was ashes. Does anybody else really feel death the way I do? Bernie does. When you don't believe in anything, death takes on a whole new dimension. Life is crazy enough...But death? Holy shit! Holy holy shit! Gone...done...out of order...finished, never to breathe, talk, smell flowers, watch birds, love, hate, get tired, get disgusted, eat, drink, play, wander, wonder, listen to music, get bored, look at the sky, go to the toilet, chew, scratch, wash, put on deodorant, make love, kiss, feel another person's body, feel your own, think, get dressed, get undressed, go to bed, wake up...none of this, ever ever again...Dead. Really dead. I love the idea of a beautiful resurrection, of the stone rolling away and beautiful Jesus floating up to heaven and, after hanging out there for a while, coming back to save the world. It's a great idea...But I don't believe it. Not for one second. I wish I did believe it. Daddy's funeral would have been easier. Much easier. But I don't believe it. But that's what makes this life so beautiful. The ugliest thing creates the most beautiful thing...Only death gives meaning to life...That kind of thing...O Daddy, I love you!

And do you know the last thing Daddy said to me? I remember it like two minutes ago..."Laura, live...Live and try to find a way to love this life. Respect the world. Respect other people. But don't let anyone tell you how to live your life."

That was it. That was the last time we talked. Then he put himself to sleep and never woke up.

No, I don't have to go anywhere. I just didn't want to talk to Johnny anymore. I had heard enough. People can make me a little sick. I can respect them, but they still can make me a bit nauseous. I leave them alone, can't they leave me alone? I don't tell anybody what to do. I don't tell anybody who to love, what to love, how to love. Why should anybody tell me? I don't tell people what to do with their precious lives before they die. They shouldn't tell me what to do with mine.

But Johnny told me the truth. People are talking. People think a teacher and his student shouldn't be loving each other. But what do these people know? Nothing. At least nothing about my life and the life of the man I love. They might think they do, but they don't. They have absolutely no idea where our love came from. They have no idea how we love and why we love and what the word "love" means to us. To judge Bernie and me is typical human bullshit. Johnny didn't bullshit me. He just reminded me of all the crap flying through the air that I want to avoid.

That was last Thursday. Today is Sunday. Sundays are odd days in Switzerland. Hardly anybody goes to church in the year 2012. It's interesting how people don't go to church, but they still believe in all kinds of ridiculous things. Like Obama. People here think he's some kind of a new Jesus. A recent survey said 98% of all Swiss voters would vote for Obama. 2% for Romney. The longer I live the more I think the press is a joke. The ghettos of America haven't gotten any better. Guantanamo is still open. Afghanistan is still a mess. He's sent four times more drones out in four years than Bush did in eight years. But they love him. They love his smile and his walk. His talk. They love him like a Will Smith and a Brad Pitt rolled into one.

No, Sunday is definitely not the Lord's day, not the good Lord who worked for six days to build the world and then rested on the seventh. The only thing my friends rest from is having gone out Saturday night until five o'clock in the morning and getting completely blasted on alcohol, Redbull, drugs, and mind-numbing music. The city of Lausanne is the party capital of French-speaking Switzerland. Most of my friends sleep until three in the afternoon on Sundays. People who don't party Saturday night wake up early and have no place to go because the stores are all closed. Of course I'm exaggerating. They have lots of places to go – like to the mountains to ski or sled or hike, to the lake to stroll or throw bread to ducks, to the cinema, to a bowling alley, museum or mini-golf. But many people say they don't

like Sundays because…because…because why? I guess
because it throws them off their routine, their Monday to
Saturday routine.

Today I won't see the man I love. Sundays Mr. and
Mrs. Fluckinger always do things with Ozzie and Freddie.
It's not quite November and it's snowing outside. They'll
probably head for the Jura mountains with a sled in the
trunk of the car.

So what will happen down the road? My road. Our road.
Will the director of the school call Bernie into his office
one day soon?…*Uh, Mr. Fluckinger, I've been hearing
rumors that…You know this is kind of thing can't go on
between a teacher and a student…*Will Bernie and his wife
decide to separate before the kids are grown to
adulthood?…*Bernie, I've had it. I don't love you and you
don't love me…Let's face it. We're only staying together for
the kids…Is that reason enough?…Maybe…But, I'm not so
sure anymore…Bernie, I feel like I'm wasting my life…I
want to be with Elisa…The kids will understand…they're
a year older…It's better they know the truth…*Or will
Bernie be the one to suggest it?…*I'm not sure…one is
never sure…But I want to leave the house…What? To move
in with your little cutie-pie!…She's not my little cutie-
pie…Actually you can call her whatever you want because
you have absolutely no idea what goes on between us and
what we feel together…No, I don't, and I'm glad…So I
think we should separate…*Or will they stay together until

Freddie and Ozzie are both over 18?…Or will Bernie and I stop loving each other? Who knows? Maybe his wife will suddenly feel her sexual apparatus moving in a different direction, an old direction, back toward her husband? Maybe his mind and my mind will go different directions. He could lose interest in me. I could meet another man…a younger man. He could meet a woman closer to his age? What guarantees are there in this life? Are there any? Maybe Bernie and I will decide to pack up and go to America and start a new life? Or to southern France, or Italy, or Japan? I've always wanted to go to Japan. Maybe I'll want to go alone…alone into outer space…or inner space…or no space…

Holy, holy world. Who the hell knows what will happen? For now…at this moment…only three things are certain in Laura Jezabel Winger's life…a) she loves absolutely everything about Bernie Fluckinger; b) Bernie Fluckinger loves absolutely everything about her, and c) when her Daddy said, "Don't let anyone tell you how to live your life," she listened. Then Daddy died.

36

I was tempted to stop the book at the end of Chapter 35. Doesn't everything have to stop somewhere, sometime? I thought I might as well leave everything up in the air. Isn't everything always up in the air. Isn't that why humans have gods…to give them certainties to hold onto! But gods are no more certain than love….

And I had to tell you what happened last Sunday. Bernie and his family didn't go to the mountains to sled. They didn't go to the zoo or a museum. His wife came to the breakfast table and announced that she was going to take the kids to go see her parents in Sion. She asked Bernie if he wanted to go. He graciously declined saying he had to correct tests. She said they wouldn't be back until dinnertime. Bernie and I finally had a chance to have a day together.

I had wondered if we were so on fire because we never spend more than a couple of hours together and every second is precious and so the flame never has a chance to die down. Yesterday we were together from from 10:30 until 6:30. Eight hours. Alone, together. I'm not stupid. I know eight hours isn't a year, a silver wedding anniversary, or a lifetime. But it was four times longer than we had ever been alone together before.

What happened? The only thing I can clearly say is that it feels like Bernie and I hatched out of the same egg.

It feels like everything in our lives led up to our coming together. It really is as if we are entwined and form one solid hunk of rope. What we experience and feel together has nothing to do with anything either of us has ever felt before. Of course he's lived longer than I have, but it's not like I was born yesterday. I've been through Marcel Monney, Cherif, Chuckie, and Johnny, all very nice people. But there was always something missing. There were always pieces of the puzzle that didn't fit. With Bernie it's different. Everything fits. It's like two planets ran into each other and became one. With Marcel, Cherif, Chuckie, and Johnny I always had this feeling that they were living in one world and I was living in another. We'd get together for a while, I'd talk about my world, they'd talk about theirs; sometimes we would make love (except with Chuckie of course…same religion as Romney…no whoopie before wedding). But we didn't make love. We made some kind of sex. With Bernie all that is different. We are always making love. Even when we're not together. Maybe I shouldn't say we make love because love is already made…We are love. I know it all sounds a little corny, but it's the only way I know how to explain it. And as far as I can tell, our relationship has nothing to do with my age or Bernie's age. He never had any intention or plan of being with me. I never saw him as a love object. I never sat in class and drooled over him. We never seduced each other. I didn't want an "older man" and he wasn't looking for a "younger woman". We just slowly, very slowly, melted together like two scoops of different ice cream at the bottom of a cup…

I couldn't stop the book after having lived what Bernie and I lived yesterday. Not only that, but the election is next Tuesday, the sixth of November, two thousand and twelve years after baby Jesus was born in a barn in Bethlehem. (At least that's what the world pretends.) Mitt and Barack have been furiously throwing their last furious set of punches. Boom! Smash! Crash! Many below the belt…Ouch! And again, not one word about the principles, thoughts, and ideas of their supposed main man, good ol' Jesus the Christ…that single solitary son of God whose life was supposed to have inspired the world-famous Christian religion. Not one peep about him out of a Mitt mouth or a Barack brain. Their view of the damn world is supposed to be based on HIM! And yet they never even say his name. In all the millions of words that have popped, fired, or slipped past their lips about what they will do to make America – and the world – a better place, there has not been one single solitary phrase about what Jesus would have done about things. There is never a question like, "Would Jesus want our army in Afghanistan?" … or maybe, "How would Jesus treat the prisoners in Guantanamo?" "Would Jesus want Americans running around with guns in their pockets?" They use the word "God" a lot. "God Bless" this and "God Bless" that. They even quote ex-Presidents and Founding Fathers. I mean nothing against guys like Georgio Washington and Tom Jefferson, but wasn't Jesus supposed to have been a little more divinely inspired than they were? At least Jesus didn't have slaves! ...Haha!... Oh well...

It is funny to compare the American presidential circus to the Swiss system. A lot of Swiss people don't even know who their president is because they have a new one every year! Here the Congress votes for seven of its members to run the country and they rotate as president every twelve months. I guess that way nobody gets a big head. And there are three or four political parties that share the power. And they get along and they compromise. And not a franc is spent on a campaign and I don't think the Swiss president even has a bodyguard. Right now there are four women and three men at the round table. A woman is about to hand the gavel to a man. And one thing is for sure, the Swiss president never says, "God Bless Switzerland!"

Since nobody wants to talk about Jesus, why would anyone care about what happens between Laura and Bernie? Who would want to know how a parentless student spent eight hours last Sunday with her teacher in a gorgeous one-hundred-and-fifty-square-meter apartment with a view of Lake Geneva and the French Alps? ... But of course you want to know. You want to know because Bernie is almost forty years old and my teacher and I am an eighteen-year-old cutie-pie with a body that looks like it just came out of the oven for Playboy magazine. Haha! You loved Clinton and Lewinsky! You'll really love Bernie and Laura! But you don't want a happy ending. You don't want Bernie and

Laura to end up skipping hand in hand down a yellow brick road. No, you want scandal! You want God throwing lightning bolts! You want Mitt and Barack beating each other to a pulp! You want Bernie fired from his job for taking advantage of a poor little defenseless motherless fatherless child! You want Monica being the victim! You want blood and guts! You don't want Jesus passing out flowers…You want the Devil throwing poison darts! You don't want peace…You want action! Isn't that what our civilization is all about? Isn't that what's really in the human heart?…

…Hey, I'm sorry. Forgive me… I get excited… Of course I don't know what you want, what you really, really want. But I do know this: I want Bernie and he wants me. We are like the Atlantic and Pacific oceans. The water isn't separate; it is "one". It's all fused together. Sure, maybe one day the water will evaporate and the oceans will separate. But for now they are united. And we are inside each other. That's the only way to describe it. Fusion…minds and bodies. Timeless time. The kingdom of God is within… here … now… heaven… on earth.

37

It's Halloween. It's also Hurricane Sandy. She's tearing up the East Coast of the United States. Wednesday, October 31. There's "Sandy", in big red letters on top of the TV screen: "SANDY ON CNN". The crowd loves it. Sandy, a film star. Sandy, a rock star. Sandy, as big as Michael Jackson when he lived and died.

Death has been on my mind all day. It must be the reaction to Sunday with Bernie. The yin-yang. The ding-dong dialectic. Sunday in paradise with Bernie and today all I can think about is death. Love-death… Bing-bang…

The death crap started in German class this morning. The teacher is a nice man. He cares about his students. He loves the German language. He will die, I thought. Languages die. Latin is dying. Ancient Greek is dying. How many languages have died since people started talking? Will German die one day? We're reading Goethe's book, "The Sorrows of Young Werther". Werther kills himself when he realizes he'll never be able to be with Charlotte, the woman he loves who is married to an older man named Albert. Charlotte tells Werther she will never leave Albert. Werther shoots himself. Bang. The teacher said Goethe wrote the book when he was about 25, but later in life he said he didn't like the ending. Good for Goethe. Would I kill myself if I couldn't be with Bernie? Would Bernie if he couldn't be with me?

Biology class. Human hearts. We watched one at work in 3D on Youtube. Miracle on Main Street. O my Lordy Lord. What a world wonder! But all hearts eventually stop. One day we all die. Merry-go-round of life and death.

French class. Flaubert. "L'éducation sentimentale". Mr. Shurter is passionate about Flaubert. I finished the book in a week. Life is deception. Disappointment. The hero sees death coming. Most exciting moment on the steps of a whorehouse as a teenager. Anticipation. Heart a tambourine. The rest of life is downhill. I have Bernie. He has me. I love him more and more every time I see him. Maybe Flaubert never had love. Maybe he never met the right woman. Never met love until death did him part. What the hell do I know? …

English class. Bernie's class. We're still reading John Cheever stories. Bernie says they're dying, waning in popularity in America. But they're not dead yet. He is trying to keep them alive for us. I listen to his voice. "Before John Cheever died, he…." I think of the other students thinking about us. Who in this world doesn't love a scandal? What news is hotter than the scandalous? Even right here in little Lausanne…

Home. Bernie couldn't come by after school. The television is on. SANDY ON CNN. Look at humanity loving seeing death. The more the merrier. Imagine a world with only love, life, and happiness – a world with no death and catastrophe. Is it death that makes love what it is?

38

Late Thursday afternoon. Almost six. He just left. He didn't get here until four-thirty. The director of the school had called him into his office… finally…

Mr. Fluckinger, I've waited as long as I can before talking to you.

Are you sure? You could have not talked to me at all.

This is no time to be joking.

I'm not joking. Maybe you don't need to talk to me at all.

I'm not so sure.

Then let's talk and find out.

You know the rumors. They're all over the school.

There's paint all over the school too.

Mr. Fluckinger, let's get to the point.

Your point or my point? I doubt we have the same points.

Don't play with me.

How about if we don't play with each other.

Mr. Fluckinger, you have been seen on many occasions going into Laura Winger's apartment building.

There are seven other apartments in Laura's building.

Are you telling me that when you go into Miss Winger's building you are not going to see her?

I didn't say that.

Then what did you say?

I just said that there were seven other families of people I could be going to visit.

And do you go visit those other people?

No.

So you visit Miss Winger.

No, I don't "visit" Miss Winger.

Then what do you do?

It's none of your business.

I decide what is and is not my business.

Don't we all.

Mr. Fluckinger, this is a serious matter. Miss Winger is your student. She lives alone. You're a married man…

Me being married has nothing to do with anything. You're married. Does that have anything to do with where you go? Actually I'm sure it does…

Don't presume, and stop beating around the bush.

You planted the bush…

So tell me why you go to Miss Winger's apartment…

Because I think she is the finest person I know on this earth and for me not to go to her apartment would be a crime against humanity.

I have the feeling you're serious.

Of course I'm serious. This is the most serious subject I know.

You see her at school. Why do you see her outside of school?

If I were the most wonderful person you knew, would you be satisfied with just seeing me at school?

You are not my student.

What does that have to do with anything?

Everything. Teachers and students cannot have certain kinds of relationships.

What "kinds" of relationships are you talking about?

You know exactly what I'm talking about.

And that's exactly the kind of relationship Miss Winger and I don't have.

What kind of relationship do you have?

We share the world.

What parts of the world do you share?

Probably parts you know nothing about.

You're trying my patience, Mr. Fluckinger.

You're trying mine.

Mr. Fluckinger, have you had sexual relations with that girl?

Now Miss Winger is "that girl". You sound like the guy who was interrogating Bill Clinton about his relationship with Miss Lewinsky.

And he finally admitted to a sexual relationship…

That was his problem. Sex is for people who don't share the world. Sex is for people who aren't in love.

So you're saying you're in love with Miss Winger?

I didn't say that. I said sex is for people who aren't in love. Clinton didn't love Lewinsky. He just wanted her for sex. That was as obvious as a full moon.

We're not here to talk about Clinton and Lewinsky. Mr. Fluckinger, just answer my question, once and for all. Have you had sexual relations with Miss Winger?

No, but it is possible that I love her more than any

person I've ever known.

And I presume she feels the same way about you.

I think that might be true.

And in spite of that you don't have sexual relations?

No.

You're telling me the truth.

Yes.

Mr. Fluckinger, I suggest you stop going to Miss Winger's apartment.

I suggest you stop calling me into your office for things that you know nothing about.

If you're lying Mr. Fluckinger, you're in big trouble.

Maybe you're the one who is in trouble. Actually, I shouldn't presume anything.

I presume you've understood me.

Without a doubt...

39

remember when you talked to me after class about that
paper i wrote on hemingway
    of course i do
    i think that s when i first fell in love with you
    really   it took a little longer for me
    how long
    about this long
    that s not very long
    actually i think i was in love with you from the first time
i saw you   but teachers aren t supposed to fall in love with
their students so i kind of shut down the machine   what i
couldn t understand was why all the boys in the class weren
t in love with you
    o bernie   i m not special
    let me be the judge of that
    okay
    we're all judges   that s all people do is judge
    okay   i judge you and i love you
    me too
    bernie   i wonder if i could live without you
    of course you could you lived without me before we met
    that s true   i did   and vice versa   but now we
know each other
    that s the danger and the beauty of the thing called
"love"

i hadn t known it until now

you know laura   i love your apartment too

*i really haven t changed anything since my father died
i just gave his clothes away to the salvation army
everything else is the same i did keep one of his sweaters
an old brown one with holes in the sleeves   he used to wear
it whenever he wasn t going to work*

what do you think you ll do in life

love you

besides that

*i have no idea   you know   i probably really would
never have to work if i didn t want to   dead parents can
be worth a lot of money   my situation is ridiculous but i
didn t ask for it*

prince william has the same kind of deal

i m glad i m not prince william

*i m gladder you re not prince william   i never thought
it was possible to love somebody like i love you   i had
really kind of given up on love*

*i m too young to have started to give up   but i was
starting to have my doubts   so bernie   what happened
with the director*

*he asked me if i had had sexual relations with you   i
said no*

so you lied to him

*of course not   i told him the exact truth   i ve never felt
like we ve had sex   what we do is way beyond that   when
you love someone what you do together is not about sex*

it s about love   i told him clinton and lewinsky had sexual
relations   but not us   he didn't ask me if we d make love
had he done so i probably would have said we don't make
love we are love

   i m not sure what you said would hold up in court

   that would depend on who the judge was   if he or she
had ever loved we'd be fine

   o bernie

   o laura

40

It's an insane world. But it's the only one we have. And now, right here in my adopted home town – lovely Lausanne, Switzerland – gossipy trash is being whispered about Bernie and me. The word is out; the geese are gawking…Can you imagine?…He's almost forty and she's eighteen!…He's only using her!…He's got to be screwing her!…She's his student!…He's her teacher!…She's too young!…He's married!…For God's sake, she's an orphan looking for a father!…He could be her father!…The lucky dirty son of a bitch!…They're going to get caught!…Get caught? Get caught doing what? Being in love? Loving? Is that what we'll get caught for? Importing too much love to the earth? Loving like no two other people I know love each other? Why don't people shut up when they don't know what they're talking about? (If that were the case, I guess most people would never talk.) No one out there has any idea what is going on between Bernie and me. No one understands one iota about what we share. No one has a clue about what we feel. But they talk. They bark. They squawk. Sometimes I hate the world. No, I don't. It's nobody's fault. You can't hate innocence. Daddy always said that nobody asked to be stupid. No, I could never hate the world. Sometimes I just want a vacation from it, to fly fly away…anywhere…anywhere in Liebeland…

41

It's election day. Did I vote? Who would I have voted for? Obama? Every kid in my school would have voted for him. Every teacher would have too, except maybe Bernie. But they can't vote. They're not American. The world wants Obama. By a landslide. Except the people who get hit by drones. Poor Romney. It must be that haircut. No match for Obama's smile. Do I care who wins? Not really. I have no idea who would be better for the world.

Bernie was in a strange mood in class today. He seemed melancholic. He rarely gets that way. Normally he has the energy of a five-year-old. We didn't get to see each other during the weekend, but it was more than that. He suddenly stopped talking about John Cheever and started talking about writers and writing in general. He asked question after question and gave no answers. The students stayed silent, but I could tell they were listening. They could see he was "out there"…in some kind of zone…*So think about it…*he said…*Why do people write? Anything? Anybody? Have you ever asked yourself that question? Why did cavemen first start scribbling on walls? Why do we write murder mysteries and love poems? Where did writing come from? Where did language come from? Who invented the first alphabet? Just think of all the alphabets humans have come up with…Do words describe the real world? What is the difference between a written* *word and a spoken word? What is the real world? Are words more or less real than what they're trying to describe? "real"? Are words grains of sand that pop from human mouths and disappear into an unfathomable sea?...unfathomable sea of what? Forgetfulness? Death? Nothingness?... Or do words actually stick to something? Do they correspond to what people like to call "reality"? Are words like Lego blocks that build up and crash down? Why did Hemingway write? Cheever? Was it a way to keep from going crazy? Were they simply talking to themselves? Did they want to change the world? Change themselves? Change a few select readers? Commune with a few select readers?...Why are Nobel Prize-winning writers so lacking in humor?..They're almost all as serious as death...Is life that serious? Shouldn't writing give us a break from seriousness? Is language that serious? Is the human condition that serious?... Does a writer's writing reveal the depths of his soul? What is a soul? Is the "soul" all the words he writes, the thoughts he thinks, and the feelings he feels? Why have there been more men writers than women? Is it because men masturbate more than women? Is writing simply masturbation? Getting things out of the head that need to be set free? Are writers simply volcanoes and geysers that have to explode? Is writing about power? About trying to become eternal? How many great writers have never been published? How many great writers just threw their stuff in the wastebasket because they knew nobody would ever read what they wrote the way they wrote it? ... How long is the book of life? If you take all the words in all the books ever written and lay them out in a line, how many times will that line go around the earth? Will it reach the moon? Mars? Jupiter? The sun? Is it all futility? Was Shakespeare right when he said, 'life is a tale as told by an idiot full of sound and fury signifying nothing'? ... Is it possible to think without words? Are emotions always connected to words? Is it possible to be intelligent without reading a single solitary book? The American Indians had no books – weren't some of them among of the finest people ever to have lived on this earth? Why are we reading books in English class? Should we be listening to Bob Dylan or the Beatles instead? Should we be listening to ghetto rap? To opera? Maybe we should be reading children's books or comic books? Might "Winnie-the-Pooh" be one of the most profound books ever written? Do writers kill themselves at a higher rate than the rest of the population? Didn't Hemingway blow his brains out? Didn't Cheever drink himself to death? Why do so many people like crime novels? Why do they want to know who killed whom and why? Is love the only thing that can compete with death in literature? Are death and love not the two main themes of all writing? Can literature tell us what love is? What death is? Can literature tell us what anything is? Can literature open a reader's mind? Maybe reading closes minds? Do minds only read what they already know?...*

He finally stopped, stared out the window, then slowly walked to his desk and sat down. Nobody made a sound. After a few moments he turned and looked at the clock behind him on the wall. There were ten minutes left before the bell would ring. He told us he had nothing more to say, but that we could do whatever we wanted to as long as we stayed in our seats and didn't make a lot of noise. He sat slumped in his chair looking straight ahead. He took a plastic green toothpick out of his pocket and started picking at his teeth. Little by little the students began to jabber. Within a minute or two the classroom sounded like a tree full of birds. When the bell rang, the chatter mixed with books being thrown into bags, then it all headed for the door. We had gym class. Only Natasha said goodbye to Mr. Fluckinger. As I walked out I turned my head and looked at him. He saw me. We knew.

42

That evening Bernie told his wife that he was going to go to the election parties in Geneva, the all-night affairs where the Republicans are in one hotel and the Democrats in another. Everybody eats and drinks, watches and waits, then cheers or sighs as the results come in from across the ocean. He said he wanted to observe Americans up close. She didn't care. He thinks she's happier when he isn't home.

He did go to Geneva. He just didn't stay very long, because he had a date with me. A little before midnight I heard his steps on the stairwell. I had the door open before he had a chance to knock. His hair and face were wet. It was raining and he never carries an umbrella.

The only thing he said about the parties was that the Republican men wore more neckties than the Democrats and the Republican women had higher heels on their shoes and their lipstick tended to be redder. He opened a bottle of wine that I had brought up from the remains of Daddy's stash in the cellar. We sat on the couch. I asked him about his monologue in school that morning. He said he wasn't sure where it came from or what had brought it on. But he didn't regret it.

The television was off. There was no music on the stereo. We stopped talking and started kissing. Other than the noise our bodies made, the only sounds came from an occasional car passing on the wet road below.

I set a leg across his lap and he rubbed it. I was wearing an old pair of jeans. When I took them off I was in the bedroom and he was in the bathroom. I heard a bell in a church tower ring once.

At six, Bernie got dressed and went home. We both had school to go to. No one will ever know how we made love.

43

I've decided to end the book here. I've said enough. I can go on living without having to tell people about it.

You all know who won the election in America. Four more years for Obama in the big white house. You'll all be informed about the next mass murder in America, or elsewhere. You'll know about deadly earthquakes and hurricanes. You'll get piles of information on your phones, TVs, and computers about wars, crashes, crooked politicians, climate change, media stars marrying, divorcing, beating each other up, fucking or screwing somebody one way or another. But you'll never know what really happened to anybody, including Bernie and me. I'll just tell you this much…Johnny and Natasha are still together, Ozzie and Freddie live with their Daddy who miraculously never lost his job, and last night after dinner they helped me do the dishes.

Find out more about Jon Ferguson
and his works at his author website:
www.jonfergusonbooks.com,
where you can also sign up for updates.

Please contribute an honest online review;
it's the easiest and most supportive thing a reader can do
for an author and/or a small independent press.
editor@hugejam.com

9 781916 604247